Readers Love
SCOTTY CADE

An Unconventional Courtship

"This is probably one of the sweetest stories that I have read in a long time."
—Guilty Indulgence Book Club

"A win-win all around."
—Literary Nymphs Reviews

Wings of Love

"…a story that you will never forget."
—Fallen Angel Reviews

"…a heartfelt and very sweet romance that I couldn't put down once I started."
—Night Owl Reviews Top Pick

Final Encore

"Mr. Cade certainly knows how to write an enchanting tale with a storyline and characters that are enjoyable to read."
—Long and Short Reviews

By SCOTTY CADE

NOVELS

LOVE SERIES
Bounty of Love
Foundation of Love
Treasure of Love
Wings of Love

Final Encore

The Mystery of Ruby Lode

An Unconventional Courtship
An Unconventional Union

Published by DREAMSPINNER PRESS
http://www.dreamspinnerpress.com

THE Mystery OF RUBY LODE
SCOTTY CADE

Published by
Dreamspinner Press
5032 Capital Circle SW
Ste 2, PMB# 279
Tallahassee, FL 32305-7886
USA
http://www.dreamspinnerpress.com/

This is a work of fiction. Names, characters, places, and incidents either are the product of the author's imagination or are used fictitiously, and any resemblance to actual persons, living or dead, business establishments, events, or locales is entirely coincidental.

The Mystery of Ruby Lode
Copyright © 2013 by Scotty Cade

Cover Art by Catt Ford

All rights reserved. No part of this book may be reproduced or transmitted in any form or by any means, electronic or mechanical, including photocopying, recording, or by any information storage and retrieval system without the written permission of the Publisher, except where permitted by law. To request permission and all other inquiries, contact Dreamspinner Press, 5032 Capital Circle SW, Ste 2, PMB# 279, Tallahassee, FL 32305-7886, USA. http://www.dreamspinnerpress.com/

ISBN: 978-1-62380-563-0
Digital ISBN: 978-1-62380-564-7

Printed in the United States of America
Second Edition
April 2013

First Edition published by Silver Publishing, June 2012

As always, to Kell. Without your continued love and support, I would never allow myself the time you allow me to dedicate to chasing my dreams. I love you!

And… thanks to Ben and Jutta Counter and Michael and Tanya Trahan for mentioning their ownership in the Ruby Lode Mine over dinner and planting this entire crazy idea in my head. I can't thank you enough for taking the time to scan and send me all your turn-of-the-century documents and for filling my overloaded brain with as much information as you could gather. Your valuable input allowed me to be as accurate as possible when writing about Ruby Lode and its surroundings in this very fictional novel about a very real gold mine. You truly are the best and Kell and I love you all.

Part ONE

BOULDER COUNTY, COLORADO
TAX AUCTION
SPRING 1914

The Mystery of Ruby Lode

Chapter ONE

"SETTLE down, folks! Settle down."

The lanky auctioneer slammed a gavel on the podium, demanding silence.

When the room was again quiet, the auctioneer looked up from his perch.

"Our next piece of property is the Ruby Lode Mining Claim, designated by the surveyor general as survey number one-nine-four-five-three. The claim embraces a portion of section six, in township two North, Range seventy-one West of the sixth Principal Meridian in the Mining District and bounded and described as more particularly set forth in the patent from the United States to O.E. Jasper of record in Boulder County, Colorado. Records; said survey number one-nine-four-five-three extending one thousand five hundred feet in length along the Ruby vein or lode; the premises herein granted containing five and fifteen hundredth acres along the South St. Vrain River. The tax lien is one hundred dollars.

"Do I hear an opening bid of one hundred dollars?"

SCOTTY CADE

You could hear a pin drop in the sparsely filled town hall.

"Do I hear an opening bid of seventy-five?"

From three rows back, Frink Davis fidgeted as he and his best friend, Counter Stephens, scanned the room for any signs of activity. A hand going up, a wink, a nod, even a cough could indicate a bid. Suddenly, out of the corner of his eye, Frink saw movement, and Counter must have seen the same movement because they both turned quickly in that direction. Seated in the front row, a rugged middle-aged man wearing a brown cowboy hat leaned over and whispered something to an exceptionally broad-shouldered man wearing all black sitting right next to him. They nodded in agreement and the man wearing the brown hat brushed his hand across the brim. Counter elbowed Frink in excitement.

"Seventy-five dollars," said the auctioneer. "Do I hear eighty?"

Frink nervously watched as Counter studied the two men. Then he scanned the room again, looking for other bidders before turning to Counter and smiling. Counter raised his hand and the auctioneer nodded.

"Eighty, I have eighty dollars. Do I hear eighty-five?"

The two men in the front row turned around with surprised looks on their faces to see where the next bid had come from.

This time, the man in black shouted, "Ninety dollars."

"Ninety dollars, I have ninety dollars. Do I hear ninety-five?"

Frink's hands were beginning to shake uncontrollably, and he felt as if sweat was pouring out of each of his palms, but he held his emotions together as he prayed his best friend could make this happen.

Wait for it, Count, wait for it, wait.... But the excitement must have gotten the best of Counter because he jumped to his feet and yelled, "One hundred dollars," glaring at the men in the front row.

Frink couldn't believe his ears, and he glared at Counter, shaking his head from side to side. He leaned in and hissed, "Ninety-five, you idiot, not one hundred."

The Mystery of Ruby Lode

"One hundred dollars, I have one hundred dollars," the auctioneer yelled. "Do I hear one-ten?"

Counter smacked himself in the head. "Fuck! Did I just say…? Did I say one hundred dollars? I meant to say ninety-five." Silence again filled the hot, stuffy town hall. Frink couldn't think. In his head he kept hearing Counter's voice over and over again: *one hundred dollars, one hundred dollars*. He put his head between his legs and did his best not to pass out.

"Going once."

More silence….

"Going twice."

Again, the two men in the front row slowly turned around and glared at them, then turned back and stared straight ahead.

But still more silence….

"Sold!" The auctioneer yelled as the gavel hit the top of the podium. "Ruby Lode sold to the gentleman in the third row."

Frink would have sworn his heart was going to leap out of his chest. Just then Counter threw his calloused hands in the air and shouted, "Hot dog, Frink, we just bought ourselves a mine."

Frink stood up with a concerned look on his face. "Count, I sure hope there's gold in that there mine, 'cause if there's not, my paw and everybody I borrowed money from to buy it is going to hang me from a tall tree with a short rope."

Frink felt Counter's hands on both of his shoulders, and his heart began to race.

"Relax, Frink, there's gold. I can just feel it. We'll find gold in Ruby Lode, or we'll die tryin'."

Frink's bottom lip quivered. "That's what I'm afraid of, and I sure hope it's not the latter."

Frink had never been able to deny his best friend anything, no matter how big or how small. All through school, Counter had gotten him into so many tight jams he'd lost track. And he'd lost count of the number of times he went home from school with bruised knuckles because he'd taken the blame for something Counter had done. The schoolmaster had vowed to break Counter's bad ways and all the while, Frink kept on covering for him.

He felt Counter's comfortable hands patting his back, and he started to calm just a little. But as quickly as those hands were there, they moved, and Frink suddenly found himself being dragged to the front of the town hall, he assumed to pay for their new gold mine. Midway to the cashier, the two rugged men from the front row stepped into the aisle and blocked their way.

"Howdy and congratulations, son," one of the men said to Counter.

Counter stood up straight and smiled. "Much obliged."

"The name's Thomas, Hepp Thomas," the man said with a slight smile while sticking his hand out in an offer of introduction. "And this here's Shull Johnson"—pointing to his friend.

"I'm Counter Stephens," Counter said as he looked hesitantly at Frink.

"And I'm Frink Davis."

Frink watched Counter accept the stranger's hand and shake; then he did the same. But the stranger held on to Frink's hand a little longer than normal protocol, looking directly into his eyes. The stranger then released him and turned to Counter.

"Good to meet you, boys," Hepp offered.

Frink looked at Counter and then the waiting cashier. "Ain't aimin' to be rude, gentlemen, but we got a little business to take care of."

"Uh, call me Hepp, and about that—before you pay the cashier, can we talk some business?"

Frink saw another cautious look fill Counter's eyes.

"What kind of business might that be?" Counter asked suspiciously.

"How would you like a couple of partners in Ruby Lode?"

Frink threw Counter a questioning glance. "Partners?"

The Mystery of Ruby Lode

"Yep," Hepp replied. "We came here to buy Ruby Lode, but we only had ninety dollars between the two of us."

Frink rubbed his head. *Boy, I know what that feels like.*

"I don't think so," Frink heard Counter tell the stranger.

He jammed his finger in Counter's side and Counter yelped. "What's that for?"

He shushed him with a wave of his hand. "Counter, can I have a word with you?"

Counter stared at Frink and waited for him to speak.

"In private," Frink ground out through clenched teeth. "Please give us a minute, gentlemen." Frink grabbed Counter's arm and escorted him outside.

When they reached the porch of the town hall, he stood with his hands on his hips. "What in tarnation do you think you're doing?"

"What do you mean, what am I doing?" Counter snapped. "I'm protecting our investment and keeping us from going into business with two thugs we just met."

"But Count, that's fifty dollars," he whined. "I could give some of the money back that I borrowed, and we could still have the mine. Come on, if that mine is half as full of gold as you say it is, there's more than enough for all of us."

"You've got a point, Frink, but we don't even know these guys. How do we know they're not going to shoot us, bury our bodies, and take our deed?"

"The mine will be in our names, and if and when we hit gold, we'll put half the mine in their name. If he doesn't agree, we try something else, but I don't want to pass up that money." Frink studied the all-too-familiar look on Counter's face that appeared when he was ciphering on something. He finally used what worked every time: his pleading eyes.

"Oh, okay, fine," Counter snapped. "But I'm not gonna give it to them too easily. And if they double cross us, I'm the one who's gonna hang you from a tall tree with a short rope." Counter gave him a warning look. "Right after I plant my boot in your ass."

Counter turned and stormed back into the town hall without waiting for his response, and Frink hurried to catch up. Hepp and Shull remained where they'd left them.

"I'm sorry, gentlemen, but—"

"What if I sweeten the pot?" Hepp quickly interjected.

"I'm listening."

Frink cleared his throat and gave Counter a stern look.

"I mean, we're listening."

Frink folded his arms. "That's better."

"Shut up and let the man talk, Frink."

"What do you have for equipment?"

"We've got what we need," Counter snapped defensively.

"Is that so?" Hepp asked. "Do you have poppet heads and winches?"

"Uh no, not yet, but—"

"Do you have rails, ore carts, picks, cold chisels, and lanterns?" Shull interrupted.

Counter's eyes got big as saucers, and Frink did his best to hide his shock. He wasn't about to give away how completely unprepared they were. They had little more than a few picks and some worn chisels.

"Shull and I have all the tools we'll ever need to break this mine," Hepp informed them. "This is not our first time at the rodeo. We're experienced miners."

Frink glanced at Counter. "Under one condition," he said.

Looking a little distrustful, Hepp said, "Okay, we're listening."

"The mine stays in our name until we hit a vein and strike it big. Then we put the mine in all our names."

Shull looked back and forth between Counter and Frink. "No deal," he said, and then turned to his partner. "Hepp, I told you this was

The Mystery of Ruby Lode

a stupid idea. Let's go." Shull headed for the door. He looked over his shoulder and added, "These boys are amateurs and we don't have time for amateurs."

"Sorry to have wasted your time, boys," Hepp said, tipping his hat in their direction. "Good luck with Ruby Lode."

Hepp turned and walked away. It was Counter's turn to poke Frink in the ribs. "We need those tools, Frink. Stop him. I think they're on the up-and-up."

Frink rolled his eyes and sighed, "I sure hope you're right. Hepp, wait."

Hepp stopped and turned around.

"Okay. You get twenty-five percent ownership right now and the other twenty-five percent when we strike it big."

Hepp turned around again and started for the door.

"Okay, okay, you win," Frink conceded. "Fifty percent right now for fifty dollars in cash."

Hepp smiled genuinely. "I'm not interested in winning. I'm interested in what's fair." Hepp went out to the porch and joined Shull. Frink and Counter followed, the four men shook hands, and just like that, they were in business together.

After paying for their new gold mine, the four new Ruby Lode mine owners walked down to the local watering hole to seal the deal. They shared a bottle of whiskey and started to get to know one another. Frink and Counter explained they shared a room over the post office in Boulder, and they'd saved every penny they could, borrowing the rest from family to buy Ruby Lode. Hepp and Shull, both single men, explained they owned a farm together in Lyons, just seven miles outside of town in the opposite direction, and they'd had moderate success mining both gold and silver over the years.

With the whiskey slowly loosening tongues, Frink listened with interest as Hepp confessed he and Shull had met an old drunk at this very saloon who had told them his family owned Ruby Lode up until the state seized the mine for back property taxes owed. Hepp told the story of how he and Shull had pumped the old guy full of whiskey, and over the course of a few hours, the guy admitted he and his grandfather had first started mining the lode in 1906. When they dug the first shaft into the mine, they had seen gold in Ruby Lode. The old cuss also explained they hadn't been able to afford the equipment needed to dig and stabilize the first shaft properly, but they had kept digging as best they could, resulting in a dangerously unstable shaft at a pretty steep thirty-degree angle. Mining the shaft was difficult and risky, but they knew there was gold so they kept going. At one point they hit what they assumed was the tip of a major vein and pulled enough gold out of the shaft to buy the equipment they needed to dig and properly shore a second shaft, hoping to hit the gold midvein. Unfortunately, they never hit that vein, but that old man swore the gold is there. Before he could find the vein, his grandfather passed away, and his family lost the mine to the state. He never told anyone about the gold, hoping one day he'd find a way to get the mine back, but he never did.

Frink watched Counter's eyes grow wide with excitement while listening to Hepp and Shull's story. When they were finished, Frink confessed he and Counter had first become interested in the mine after hearing the identical tale from the same old man.

"That old man gets around," Frink chuckled. "Wonder how many more people he's told his story to?"

"Doesn't really matter none." Hepp raised his glass in salute before taking a sip. "The mine belongs to us now."

"Let's just hope the old guy is right about the gold." Shull shook his head. "We're all betting on it."

Suddenly the table got quiet, and their moods took a somber turn. Probably a combination of the whiskey and the shared admission that they'd each spent their last penny based on the ramblings of an old drunk bellied up to this very bar.

Counter downed his last shot of whiskey and closed his eyes as he enjoyed the slight burn. "Well, if he's not right, we're all doomed."

With the getting-to-know-you phase clearly out of the way and the celebratory mood over, the realization of what they'd just done

The Mystery of Ruby Lode

began to set in. Frink's right knee started to bounce, and goose bumps ran up and down his spine. He was suddenly very anxious about the days ahead and ready to get started. The four men quickly made plans to meet the next morning at Hepp and Shull's farm to get the needed equipment. They'd take the equipment up to Ruby Lode and at the same time, survey the shafts for safety and stability. After saying his goodnights, each man left looking forward to getting to work on the mine.

The next morning, following the directions given to them, Frink and Counter rode the seven miles or so to Hepp and Shull's farm, and together they loaded what equipment they could fit into Hepp's wagon and departed for the two- to three-hour ride to Ruby Lode. When they arrived, the four men stood at the base of the mountain and looked up at an almost vertical peak. There stood the capped entrance to their new mine. The capping was a ten foot by twenty foot platform with a shed roof built over the mine's opening.

Frink looked up the mountain in disbelief. "How in the hell are we going to get the equipment up there?"

Shull gave him a knowing glance and a jab to the ribs. "The same way we'd get ore, or in our case, gold, out of the mine: by pulley system."

Frink eyed the heavy equipment with uncertainty. "Hope you have some mighty strong rope," he commented with a shrug.

Hepp suggested he and Counter unload the equipment while Frink and Shull climbed up to the mine's entrance with ropes and pulleys over their shoulders. The climb was slow going, but the last hundred yards were the toughest. Frink and Shull crawled up the almost vertical peak on all fours, mostly holding on to vegetation to keep them from sliding back down the mountain. When they reached the mine's entrance, Frink watched as Shull secured the pulleys to a large rock covered by the old wooden structure protecting the mine's opening. He slipped ropes through each one and told Frink to stay put.

"I'm going to lower myself back down the mountainside with the ends of the ropes. No sense both of us risking our lives," Shull teased and winked.

Frink sat on the large rock and stretched his legs out. "Be my guest. I'll gladly sit right here and watch ya work."

Frink gasped when Shull lost his footing and started sliding down the mountain before digging his boots in and stopping his descent downward. He let out the breath he didn't know he was holding when Shull gave him a weak smile and thumbs up before continuing down the mountain. He watched anxiously until Shull finally reached the bottom. Shull, Counter, and Hepp secured item after item to the ropes and hoisted the equipment slowly but surely to Frink's awaiting arms. He stacked and organized the equipment as it came up, and just as the sun dipped over the mountain, the full wagon of equipment had been completely hoisted up and organized. Frink stretched his overworked back before heading down to join the others.

HEPP stood and wiped the sweat from his brow with his red work handkerchief. "One more load tomorrow and that should do it." He shoved the handkerchief into his back pocket. "No need for you boys to ride the fifteen miles back home when you can just follow us and stay at our place. It's nothing special, but it's clean. Shull can cook up a mess of something and y'all can spend the night. That way we can get an early start in the morning."

Frink looked at Counter, and he nodded his head in agreement. The sooner he filled his belly and laid his head down for the night, the better.

"That'd be mighty fine, Hepp," Frink said appreciatively. "Much obliged."

When they again reached Shull and Hepp's farm, Hepp, Frink, and Counter tended to the horses while Shull went into the house and

The Mystery of Ruby Lode

rustled up something for them to eat. Soon, all four men were cleaned up and sitting down to a dinner of hearty beef stew and warm bread.

Frink took a bite of warm buttered bread. "This is awful good."

"I'll say," Counter added. "Where'd you learn to cook like this, Shull?"

"I was born back east, and my momma died when I was thirteen. I had two younger brothers and my daddy had to work, so that left only me to take care of the young'uns," Shull explained. "You do what you gotta do to get by, so I had no choice but to learn."

Counter and Frink watched as Hepp gave Shull a warm smile in an almost proud but loving way.

"Wow, Shull," Counter added. "That couldn't have been easy."

"'Tweren't easy. But nothing worth nothing in life is—easy, I mean," Shull admitted. "I did what I had to do to give my brothers the best chance I could give them. Hell, I was their maw and paw all rolled up into one most of the time. Especially the youngest. He was only a year old when Maw died."

Counter had a confused look on his face. "How did you know how to take care of a young'n?"

"I'd watched my Maw with both babies and did mostly what she did. Pretty soon I learned if you keep them fed and clean, most of time they're pretty happy, unless they're sick or something."

Hepp cleared the dishes and they all pitched in until everything in the tiny kitchen was clean and organized.

Frink stretched and yawned. "Where do you want us to sleep?"

Hepp looked at Shull with a questioning look and Shull nodded.

"There's an extra bedroom upstairs next to ours if you boys don't mind sharin'."

It was Counter and Frink's turn to look at each other.

Frink's eyes widened. "You men sleep together?"

"Yep, for the last twelve years," Shull confessed. "You got a problem with that?"

"I… I guess not," Frink stammered uneasily. "You boys sodomites?"

"That's not a term we like to use," Hepp said with distaste. "But yep, I guess so."

Up to this point, Counter hadn't said anything. Frink watched as he rocked from one foot to the other, nervously looking back and forth from Frink to Hepp to Shull.

"Counter?" Shull asked. "You have anything to say?"

"Uh, no, sir, just shocked is all. Never met a real sodomite before."

"Sure you have, son, you just don't know it. This is not something we talk about with many folks. Our ways are not popular with most people, so we keep to ourselves."

"But you guys don't seem like sodomites," Frink said curiously. "I mean, you're big, strong, and manly. Everyone thinks sodomites wear dresses and have pretty hair and act like girls."

Hepp and Shull both laughed at that one. "How old are you boys?" Hepp asked.

"I'm nineteen."

"And I'm twenty," Counter added.

"The way you describe what we are is what most people think when they think of sodomites, so no one ever suspects us," Hepp said. "We've lived here for going on eight years and no one we know has ever questioned our manhood. We don't rub our lifestyle in folks' faces and everyone leaves us alone."

"Are you afraid of burning in Hell?" Counter blurted.

Hepp looked at Shull before turning a questioning look toward Counter. "Why do you think we're going to burn in Hell?"

"When I was a kid, I remember our preacher in church preaching about Sodom and Gomorrah and how all sodomites would eventually burn in Hell for their sins. He said sodomy ain't natural and is against God."

The Mystery of Ruby Lode

"Son, faith is faith, and Hepp and me, we live good, clean lives. We ain't done nothing against God. Besides, if he sends us to Hell for loving one another, then his Heaven is not a place we want to be anyway."

Hepp continued before Frink or Counter could respond. "You boys are going to believe what you want to believe, so filling your head with our beliefs won't do anyone any good."

"Look," Shull interrupted. "The only reason we said anything at all is because we felt that if we were going to be in business together, we wanted to be honest with you. That's all."

"Much obliged," Frink said. "I don't personally believe all that fire and brimstone talk, and I don't really know where sodomites go when they die, but faith aside, it's not for me to say what two people do behind closed doors." Frink looked at Counter, hoping he wouldn't continue down his current line of questioning.

"Yeah, what he said," Counter agreed with a curt nod.

"Then that settles it," Hepp said. "No need to bring it up ever again."

"Let me show you boys to your room," Shull motioned towards the stairs. "We need to be loaded and ready to go at first light."

FRINK and Counter stripped and crawled into bed like old habit. They slept in the same bed every night in their little room above the post office and had shared a bed many times before that as kids during their twelve years of friendship. Frink thought about the many times they'd had relations in the quiet of the night, starting out exploring like boys do when they were kids, but continuing on well into their young adult life. Counter had never once spoken of what they'd done, nor had he ever acknowledged the feelings Frink knew hung between them, but after both tossed and turned for quite some time, Frink was the first to speak. "Count, you awake?"

"Yep, I'm up."

"I know we've slept together hundreds of times since we were kids, but lying next to you feels different to me tonight."

"I know what you mean," Counter admitted. "Maybe it's because we're sleeping so close to sodomites."

Frink hesitated and then asked the question that had been plaguing him for so many years. "Do you think we're sodomites?"

Counter sat up in bed. "Why in tarnation would you ask that?"

"Well, because we've... uh, slept together so many times."

"That doesn't make us sodomites."

"Doesn't it?" Frink suggested.

"Heck no! You've got to do stuff," Counter insisted.

There was silence for a few minutes. "Count?"

"Yeah?"

Frink opened his mouth to speak, but thought better of it. "Uh... never mind. Goodnight."

"Goodnight, Frink."

"WELL, that went pretty well," Shull said as he snuggled against Hepp's broad chest.

"I guess so, but Counter didn't seem as okay with us as Frink seemed to be."

"Yeah, I picked up on that too."

"Shull, have you ever noticed the way Frink looks at Counter?"

"Yeah, I have. Like the sun rises and sets just to shine on him. Just like the way I look at you," Shull admitted.

"You think...?"

"Who knows, but those boys have known each other since they were kids, and we all know what kids do when they reach puberty."

The Mystery of Ruby Lode

Hepp chuckled. "I know what you mean, but I guess time will tell about those two. The more we work together and get to know each other better, maybe they'll get used to us and relax and just accept us."

"I sure hope so, 'cause I like them both. They're good boys."

"Me too. 'Night, Shull."

"'Night, Hepp. I love you."

"I love you too."

Chapter TWO

FIRST light found them loaded and ready to get moving. Frink was a little preoccupied and didn't really feel like talking, but Counter was all business. With Hepp and Shull on the wagon and he and Counter on their horses, they started the journey along the St. Vrain River to the base of the mountain. Once there, for the second day, they would unload their equipment and hoist everything up to the waiting mine. Not wanting to leave the previous day's equipment easily accessible, they'd removed the pulleys and ropes and therefore would need to set everything up again. As they'd done the day before, Frink and Shull climbed the side of the steep mountain to the waiting platform. However, unlike the day before, Frink didn't feel like talking. When they reached the entrance to Ruby Lode, they again set up the pulley system, and Frink fed the ropes as they'd done the previous day.

"You okay?" Shull asked. "You seem awfully quiet."

"Just got a lot on my mind, I guess."

"Does it have anything to do with Hepp and me telling you about our… uh… being together?"

The Mystery of Ruby Lode

Frink didn't answer right away, and suddenly he thought the silence was deafening.

"We're sorry for just coming out of the blue with it. We just felt like we wanted to be honest with you boys."

Frink started fidgeting and looked off into the distance. His palms were starting to sweat, and his heart started pounding in his chest. *Why am I so darn nervous?*

"You're starting to worry me, son," Shull admitted. "You're white as a ghost."

All Frink could do was nod, his throat suddenly dry. His heartbeat was running rapid but started to return to normal when Shull didn't push the subject any further and started getting ready to make his descent. As Shull threw his legs off the platform, unable to hold it back any longer, Frink finally spoke. "Shull, wait," he squeaked out.

Shull stopped dead in his tracks and their eyes met.

"Can I ask you something? I mean, just between us."

"Sure," he said as he climbed back up, sat next to Frink on the platform, and waited for him to get up the nerve to speak.

"How did you know?"

"How did I know what?"

"Uh… well, you know…." Frink wrung his hands nervously and whispered, "I mean about being a sodomite and all."

Shull took a deep breath and closed his eyes. "I guess I always knew. You know, kids do stuff when they're young, and some grow out of it and some don't. I was one of the ones that didn't grow out of it."

Frink hung on Shull's every word as he continued. "Before I met Hepp, I didn't act on any of my desires. Got real good at hiding it." Shull shrugged and a warm smile crossed his rugged face. "But the minute I first laid eyes on Hepp, I knew there was no way I'd be hiding my attraction, but I tried."

"How… uh, did you two meet?" Frink asked.

"Hepp and I met in our early twenties when I went to work for a family that owned and operated several gold mines in the mining district. My first day on the job, Hepp and I happened to be assigned to the same mine shaft and worked closely together for a few days. We found we worked well together and had a comfort level one only finds occasionally. On the fourth day, we were working a large section of the mine when the entrance collapsed, and we were trapped alone together."

Frink felt his eyes widen at the thought of being trapped in a mine shaft.

"For twenty-two hours, we didn't know if we were going to live or die or even if they were trying to find us or dig us out. With each passing hour, our hope diminished, and we figured that our lives were going to end right there in that mine. Hepp sensed my giving up and tried to comfort me as best he could. By the flicker of our lantern, we sat in a corner nearest the entrance and waited for our time to come. I didn't want to die without a human touch, so I rested my hand on Hepp's leg and he rested his hand on mine. The next thing we knew, we were in the heat of passion, and that passion has not failed us to this day."

"Obviously, you were rescued." Frink chuckled.

"Yeah, several hours later they broke through and we were pulled to safety." Shull paused. "Frink, why are you asking me all these questions?"

Frink again started to fidget. He wasn't ready to admit he had the same kind of desires for Counter that Shull had for Hepp, at least to anyone but himself.

"Does this have anything to do with the way you look at Counter?"

Frink jumped up and glared at Shull. "What do you mean, the way I look at Count?"

Shull ignored the venom in Frink's voice and said confidently, "It's pretty obvious to Hepp and me that there's a glimmer in your eye where Counter is concerned. Are you and Counter, you know, involved in some way?"

The Mystery of Ruby Lode

Looking defeated, Frink again sat down next to Shull and sighed. Then he whispered, "Are my feelings that obvious?"

"They kinda are," Shull admitted. "To us, anyway."

"Count's my best friend, and, dadburnit, I love him. I'd take a bullet for him, and I hope he'd do the same for me."

Shull rested his hand on Frink's leg and Frink tensed up. Shull must have sensed his discomfort because he quickly removed his hand and placed it back by his side.

"Do you love him like you love a best friend, or is there something more to it?" Shull asked with an understanding look in his eyes as if he already knew the answer.

Frink gathered up the nerve to speak. He opened his mouth once, then closed it again. Then his bottom lip started to quiver, and a single tear slid down his cheek. He opened his mouth yet again and in the lowest whisper, he said, "I've loved Count for as long as I can remember."

Frink saw Shull's expression change.

"I can't imagine what it must be like to love someone, be around them all the time, and not be able to truly have them," Shull said. "Have you told him how you feel?"

"Nah, I ain't never gonna tell him. I've tried a couple of times, but I always chicken out."

"Have you and Counter been, uh… together?" Shull asked.

"We've done stuff. It started when we were kids, but it didn't stop when we got older. It's less frequent now but still happens from time to time. Recently, it's mostly in the middle of the night when Count pretends to be sleeping, but his hands are very awake. I know he knows what he's doing, and I know he remembers everything, but we never talk about it, ever."

"I'm not sure what to tell you, son," Shull said. "Until you're ready to tell him how you feel, neither Hepp nor I can really help you."

"I want to tell him," Frink admitted. "But Count's changed over the last year. He's angrier all the time and goes off at the drop of a hat."

"Why do you think that is, son?"

"I don't really know 'cause he won't talk about it, but I think it has something to do with me or at least with us."

"What do you mean?"

"Well, up until Counter turned twenty years old, we did stuff." Frink looked at Shull and it was clear to Shull what stuff meant. "A lot. And it was good, real good, between us. Count's touch was gentle and sweet, and after it was done, we'd hold each other, but that all stopped when Counter turned twenty. It became less and less, and he became sullen. It's like, now that he's twenty, we aren't supposed to do stuff no more. As if when a man turns twenty and sleeps with another man, you're a real sodomite. No offense, Shull."

"None taken," Shull said and smiled.

"And all this is just my take on it, you know, 'cause he won't talk about it, but I think he's having a real hard time knowing he wants what we had, but now he can't have it unless he admits to himself he's a sodomite. Does that make any sense?"

"Yep, I think it makes perfect sense, and I think you're wise beyond your years."

Frink smiled sheepishly. "Thanks."

"But son, you can't change him. He's either going to accept what he is or not, and you can't do anything about that."

Defeated, Frink hung his head and whispered, "I know. I was hoping if I was patient, eventually I would see the old Counter again, the one I fell in love with."

"Give it some time, son. Maybe Counter being around Hepp and me might help him understand himself a little better. But you need to decide what you want and not leave the rest of your life up to Counter."

"Thanks. I'll give all this some thought. And… please don't tell nobody, Shull."

"I'll tell no one but Hepp. I've never kept a secret from him, and I'm not about to start now."

"Okay, just Hepp and no one else."

"Deal," Shull said as he offered his hand.

They shook hands just as Hepp called up to the mountain, "What in tarnation are you boys doing up there?"

"I'm on my way. I'll be down in a second," Shull yelled.

The rest of the day went smoothly—each man pulling his weight—and eventually all the equipment was hoisted up the mountain, secured, and ready to go.

Exhausted, they all sat on the back of the wagon and plotted out the next day. Their plan was to enter the first of the two existing mine shafts to determine the structural stability and see what reinforcements would be needed to make the shaft safe to mine. They knew from what they were told by the old man that he'd hit what he thought was the tip of a vein in the first shaft, which is why he dug the second shaft. But Hepp and Shull wanted to see the condition of the mine shaft for themselves, and Counter and Frink agreed. Their main objective was to determine whether the first shaft was worth mining at all.

Hepp and Shull started hooking the horses to the wagon in preparation for the ride home.

"If you boys want to follow us home again and spend the night, you're right welcome to," Shull offered.

Counter looked at Frink. "Much obliged, but I think we'll make our way home, if it's all the same to you."

"Suit yourself," Hepp said. "We'll leave our place at first light."

"We'll do the same," Counter promised.

Hepp climbed up onto the wagon and took the reins. "Let's git, Shull. We're losing daylight mighty fast."

"Ready," Shull said. "You boys ride safe now."

"Same to you," Frink offered.

"Getup," Hepp said as he cracked the reins, signaling to the horses they were ready to go. Shull gave one last tip of his hat as Hepp pulled the wagon onto the road and started for home.

FRINK and Counter both waved, mounted their horses, and headed in the opposite direction. The horses were sure of the route home, so that left Frink with nothing to do and plenty of time to think. *Could I dare to hope Count and me might have what Hepp and Shull have? But wouldn't Count have to at least admit we have anything at all? I've tried to talk to him about it, but I just can't seem to form the words. How long am I expected to be in love with someone who doesn't want me in that way? I think I've tortured myself long enough, but what do I say? Would you be my sodomite?* He gave himself an internal shake. *No, that won't work. Count, I'm in love with you, can we set up housekeeping together?* Frink shook his head at the way that one sounded. *No, that sounds too sissy-like. Stop it, Frink, and just speak from the heart. Tell him how you feel.* He chastised the little coward keeping him from admitting the truth to Counter. *It's either that or spend the rest of your life pining over Counter Stephens. I'll do it on the ride back up tomorrow morning. Count loves sunrise and he's always happiest watching the sun come up over the mountains.*

With that settled, Frink relaxed and realized they were nearing home.

"Welcome back," Counter chuckled. "You've been gone for quite a while."

"I'm sorry. A lot on my mind is all."

"You've been awfully quiet ever since you and Shull went up the mountain this morning. Did he try anything with you up there?"

"No!" Frink barked. He wanted to say, "I would never do anything with anyone but you," but he thought better of it. He simply mumbled, "Why would you ask something like that?"

"They's sodomites and that's what sodomites do," Counter said, rather matter-of-factly.

"I don't believe Shull would do anything of the sort," Frink snapped back.

The Mystery of Ruby Lode

"Suit yourself, but I'd keep my eye on both of them if I were you."

Frink ignored the comment and dismounted. He led his horse into the local stable with Counter right behind him. They busied themselves feeding, watering, and bedding them down for the night. Neither one said a word to the other, but the tension between them was very obvious.

Frink sat down on a bale of hay and waited for Counter to finish with his horse. Counter was whistling and humming like all was well with the world. *Look at him. It's just like him to be happy-go-lucky and not have a clue as to what's going on around him. I've lived with this for God knows how long, and he's never going to change, so why can't I just leave and start a new life somewhere else? Hepp and Shull found each other; maybe I could find someone to love me too.* Frink sighed, knowing he'd never leave Count. He loved him too much.

"Frink!"

"What?"

"Dadburnit, I called your name three times. Let's git. I'm so tired I'm 'bout to drop."

They walked in silence to the next block, where the US Post Office stood. The two men climbed the little flight of rickety stairs alongside the building, and Frink pushed open the door to their tiny room. He undressed and washed up mostly in a deep cloud of thought, and when he finally turned to get into the bed, Counter was passed out on his back, completely dressed. *God, Count, can't you even get undressed?* But Frink knew the answer to that question. When Counter was out, he was out.

He stared at Counter's six-foot-six-inch frame with a longing he hadn't felt in a while. *Why is this so darn hard all of a sudden, and why do I have this all-out need to tell him how I feel? I've been secretly in love with him for as long as I can remember, and I've dealt with it.* "Maybe because it's no longer a secret, you fool. You told Shull," Frink mumbled under his breath. *God, I told Shull. And maybe, just maybe, seeing that Hepp and Shull have a life together opened my eyes to a few things. I never knew two men could be together and not be frowned on.*

Frink took this opportunity to really look at Counter. His long blond locks were spread half across his face and half across his pillow. He couldn't see them, but he knew Counter's deep violet eyes were beautiful behind his closed lids. He studied Counter's nose, small and slender, but appropriate for the size of his face. His eyes moved lower to Counter's full, pouty lips and then his broad, square jawline. He looked regal and proud even in his sleep. Frink's gaze slid down to Counter's Adam's apple, then farther, pausing at his broad chest as it rose and fell with each breath. Then even further still, down to the bulge in his britches; he lingered there for more than a few seconds before admiring his long slender legs as they hung off the end of the bed.

Mental and physical exhaustion consumed Frink with each of his own breaths, and his need for sleep outweighed the pleasure he was feeling as he watched Counter's slow, even breaths. But before he could finally call it a night himself, he needed to take care of Counter, the way he'd always done.

He sighed and pulled off Counter's boots and socks, one by one. *How many times have I done this?* He unbuckled his belt, unbuttoned his britches, and then slid them off. He then unbuttoned his shirt slowly and deliberately. When he was through with the buttons, the fronts of Counter's shirt fell to his sides, exposing his massive chest sprinkled with curly blond hair. Frink's eyes followed Counter's chest hairs down the "V" shape to his waist, where they disappeared into his long johns. He ever so lightly used his index finger to brush the hair out of Counter's face. He then rolled him to one side and slipped one sleeve of his shirt off, then the other, and like a god, there Counter lay in only his long johns.

Frink's heart was suddenly leaping out of his chest and breaking at the same time. *I love you, Count.* He was filled with these gut-wrenching emotions that were threatening to escape him. He held it together and climbed into bed. He slid in next to Counter, as close as he could get without actually touching him. Need filled every fragment of his being, and tears started running down his cheeks. His body heaved with longing for the man lying next to him. *How can I do this for the rest of my life?* He trembled and the sobs continued.

In the midst of Frink's breakdown, Counter rolled over and threw his arm across Frink's chest, and Frink froze. He held his breath until he could control the sobs escaping him. Counter suddenly pulled Frink close to him and gently stroked Frink's face with the back of his fingers. He closed his eyes as tightly as he could to pretend this moment wasn't happening, but he knew what was coming. It had been happening since they were kids. Frink was torn between protecting his heart and the need Counter always stirred in him. *Please don't let this be happening—not tonight.*

Frink put his hand up to move Counter's hand from his face, and Counter took hold of it and held on tightly. *How can I push him away now? He must need me. And God knows I need him. Maybe just this one last time. When I tell him how I really feel, I'm sure he'll run and I'll be free of the bittersweet torture named Counter Stephens.*

Counter pushed Frink's shoulder-length straight brown hair away and snuggled into his neck, lightly kissing and nibbling. He gently ran his lips along Frink's slender but well-developed chest as he ran his hand up and down his torso, taut with muscles he'd developed by hard work, day after day, week after week, and year after year. Frink's heart raced as Counter's hand slid closer and closer to his manhood with each stroke. He felt the familiar thrusts of Counter's prick grinding against his leg, his own prick growing by the second. Apparently, Counter felt it as well because he reached down and took hold of it through Frink's underwear. Frink unwillingly thrust into Counter's grip, moving back and forth, and Counter moved right along with him. Counter slipped his hand into his long johns and took hold of his throbbing prick. Thrust after thrust into Counter's warm palm, combined with the large man gently kissing his neck, forced Frink's release.

He closed his eyes as tightly as they'd ever been and tried not to think about how he would feel when this was over. But soon his need for Counter overtook him, and he felt himself giving in to the pleasure. When he came, he tried to stifle any sound that might escape him, but he was unsuccessful, and the sounds of his momentary ecstasy filled the small room.

Frink was still trying to catch his breath when he felt Counter pull his hand out of his long johns and wipe it on the bed linens. He instinctively knew what was coming next. They'd shared this routine since puberty, and like the most predictable almanac, by the light of the moon, Counter slid down between his legs and pulled his long johns down and off. Counter raised Frink's legs in the air and spit into his hand. Counter pressed up against his opening and pushed his way in, all the way in. Frink broke out in a heavy shroud of sweat and gasped his way through the initial burn. He loved and hated this part because, as much as he longed to feel Counter inside of him, he always felt like he was being used, simply a warm, welcoming hole. Counter had never reciprocated with anything other than a hand job, and Frink thought that was simply out of an obligation so he could get what he wanted.

He placed both of his hands on Counter's thighs and did his best to control the force of the thrusts. The closer Counter came to his release, the harder and harder the thrusts became. He opened his eyes as Counter released a low, guttural moan and his violet eyes rolled into the back of his head. Counter released his load into Frink's gut, spurt after spurt until he was empty. Without as much as a word, Counter climbed off of him, rolled over, and went to sleep.

Frink turned over, facing the opposite direction with his back to Counter. There he lay, eyes wide open and staring straight at the door. At that very moment, he hated Counter with a passion and wanted to be as far away from him as possible, but he knew he could never follow through with leaving. Especially not now, since they had bought a mine together with Shull and Hepp. He owed it to them both to at least keep up his end of the bargain. And it would do no good to leave. He knew Counter wouldn't try to stop him, and in the end, he would still be

The Mystery of Ruby Lode

alone. So what was the difference? He gripped the bed linens, pulled his fists up under his chin, and forced himself to try and sleep.

But sleep wouldn't come for hours yet, just dreadful thoughts of feeling like there was no way out and it would be this way for the rest of his life. For so many years, he had covered for Counter, took the blame for stupid things they'd done as kids and into young adulthood. Frink always justified Counter's stupid behavior by telling himself he was just being mischievous and meant no real harm. In fact, he admired Counter because he had guts and backbone. And he later told himself it was just because Counter was spontaneous and full of energy and life. But in all the times he'd covered for him, Counter had never once said "thank you" or even acknowledged Frink had protected him from harm.

Tears began to stream down Frink's cheeks again, and he started to tremble. But this time he cried for himself—not for loving Counter, but because he would never be loved back. His stomach turned upside down, and he wished his heart would literally just stop beating.

If only I could just die right here in this bed with Counter my life wouldn't be in such a mess. Do I want to die? No, I don't want to die; I want Count to love me and want me. But what a complete fool I've been; that will never happen. I've wasted so many years loving a man I can never have and not feeling worthy of anything better. Damn you, Shull and Hepp, for making me see that life could be different. I can never go back to the way it's been, and the only alternative is to tell Counter how I feel about him, surely get rejected, and lose him for good. But... maybe he won't reject me. Maybe he feels the same way and was afraid to tell me for fear of the same rejection. After all, I've never had the courage to give him any signs about the way I feel. Could Counter really be that blind and not see the way I feel about him? Maybe... just maybe. Tomorrow I'll do it. I've got to tell him, and if he rejects me, I'll sign my half of the mine over to Paw and get out of town. That's the only way I can survive this.

Sleep finally took him and, although it seemed like he'd only been sleeping for a few minutes, he was awakened by Counter's cheery voice and a shake on the shoulder. Counter always loved the mornings and loved watching the sunrise of a new day. As kids, when they would spend the night at each other's farms, Count would always wake him just before sunrise and drag him outside. "Today's another day, Frink," he would say. "Full of adventure and life. Let's see what we can do with it." Counter's excitement at a mere sunrise brought a smile to his lips and made Frink love him even more. He felt Counter shake him again, and he pulled the covers up over his head.

Counter jumped on top of him and started tickling him as they'd done as kids. "Get up, sleepyhead. Today's another day full of adventure and life. Let's see if we can strike it rich in our new gold mine."

Secretly, Frink loved this drill, and he was smiling under the covers as he yelled, "Stop! Get off me, Count. I'm gettin' up."

"I'll see you at the stable."

Frink peeked his head out from under the covers just as Counter hopped off of the bed and ran through the door. He imagined him taking the stairs two by two, rushing for a glimpse of sunrise.

Frink laid there for a few minutes dreading what he knew was going to be a difficult day. *I've got to do it. I can't live like this any longer, and I deserve to be happy.*

He climbed out of bed, washed his face, dressed, and found Counter at the stables where he said he'd be. Counter had already saddled his horse and was saddling Frink's.

"I could have done that," Frink protested.

"I wanted to do it."

"Why?"

"I don't know, I just wanted to. Just get on your horse and let's get out of here," Counter ordered. "We're gonna be late."

They again rode mostly in silence. Frink knew Counter was always quiet in the mornings, enjoying the stillness and peace before the day got started. But his own silence was caused by something much deeper and something that could have a drastic conclusion. *Today's the day, Frink. Life as you know it either begins or ends. Should you do it*

The Mystery of Ruby Lode

now or should you do it on the way home? Perhaps it was better to wait until the way home. I'd hate to ruin the first day in the mine for Shull and Hepp. But I've got to be prepared for either outcome. If all went well, I could be with Count forever, but if not, I'll be starting a new life somewhere else, all alone. The thought sent a chill down his spine.

He was startled out of his thoughts by Counter's voice.

"Cat got your tongue?"

"Nah, just thinkin'."

"'Bout what?"

"Nothin' really. How'd you sleep last night?"

"Mighty fine. Don't think I even woke up once until morning."

That one statement sent Frink's heart into a tailspin and knocked the air right out of his lungs.

"How 'bout you?"

"Good," Frink managed to choke out.

"You okay?" Counter asked.

Frink cleared his throat. "Yep."

"You don't seem fine."

"I'm fine. I just want to talk to you about something later. Not now, but on the way home. Do you think we can do that?" Frink asked.

Counter appeared to be thinking. "Don't see why not. You wanna give me a clue?"

"Nah, I'd rather wait until tonight."

"Suit yourself," Counter said, "Suit yourself."

When they reached Ruby Lode, Shull and Hepp were already there. They'd left the wagon behind and rode in on horseback.

"Mornin'," Hepp said, tipping his hat.

"Mornin'," Counter and Frink said simultaneously.

"You boys have a good night?" Shull asked.

"Slept like a log," Counter admitted.

Frink winced at the admission, but held his tongue. *Why don't you just rip my heart out with your bare hand, throw it on the ground, and stomp all over it until it stops loving you?*

"You're awful quiet, Frink," Shull said.

"I'm good. Let's get this day started." He turned away from the others, more than ready for anything to keep him busy and his thoughts off Counter.

All four men climbed up to the entrance of the mine and prepared to enter Ruby Lode for the first time. They all decided it was best to enter the second shaft first, since that was probably where they would begin mining. They also agreed Hepp and Shull would take the lead as they had done all this before, and Counter and Frink would bring up the rear. They tied ropes around their waists and secured the other ends to the mine's capping. From what the old man had told them, they knew the mine was dug at a thirty-degree angle and was fairly unstable, so this was more of a reconnaissance mission to see what needed to be done to stabilize the shaft. With their leather tool bags over their shoulders and lanterns tied to their belts, one by one, Hepp, Shull, and Counter backed down the opening of the shaft and disappeared into the darkness.

At his turn, Frink positioned himself at the opening and slowly lowered himself down the shaft. It was dark, damp, and very eerie. A shiver of unease trickled down Frink's spine as he moved slowly downward. The shaft was filled with the sounds of creaks and cracks where what little support remained held the earth at bay, adding to his anxiety. Every so often, he would catch a glimpse of one of the lanterns below him, but most of the time it was pretty dark. Stray rocks, apparently loosened during the descent, would sail past his head, and he would hear one of the other guys say "shoot" or "dadburn rocks," but other than that, it was just the sound of shuffling boots against rocks and dirt.

"Shull, you okay?" Hepp called from below.

"Yep," Shull yelled. "How 'bout you boys?"

"I'm good," Counter answered.

The Mystery of Ruby Lode

"Me too," Frink added.

"I'm almost to the bottom. Just a few more feet," Hepp yelled. "Made it, I'm down. It looks pretty secure."

Shull, Counter, and Frink all ended up at the bottom of the mine in a chamber about six feet square. The chamber was strewn with picks, shovels, and a few buckets but nothing else. The scent of damp earth hung cloyingly in the small chamber, burning Frink's nostrils. Frink shined his lantern around the chamber, and the light reflecting off the smooth walls added to the smothering size of the room. Two shafts had been dug off from the main chamber.

"There," he said, pointing to the shaft at his right. "That looks like the newer one."

They entered the second shaft and found many drifts off to the left and right. He pointed to one of the other drifts, about eight feet in length, and noted that one was slightly lighter in color compared to the others, appearing as if it had been the one with the more recent activity.

Counter obviously saw the same thing Frink had seen. He pointed to the drift with the lighter coloring. "That's gotta be where the old man was digging."

Hepp and Shull both joined them, and together they slowly walked down the drift to the end.

"I think you boys are right," Hepp confirmed. "This is the logical place to start."

"Yee doggie!" Counter yelled at the top of his lungs as he kicked the walls with his boot. "We's gonna be rich!"

"Noooo," Hepp warned in a hushed tone. "No loud yelling. This thing is already unstab—"

Before he could finish his sentence, the mine started to rumble, and rocks began sliding in through the mine's opening. More and more rocks, bigger rocks, now filled the small space.

"This way," Hepp yelled, pulling Shull and diving into the back of one of the shafts at the fork. Frink instinctively grabbed Counter and followed. When they landed, without hesitation, Frink covered Counter with his body and put himself between Counter and the onslaught of debris to protect him from harm. The noise was deafening, louder and louder. The earth continued to shake beneath them, and Frink thought this was the surely the end.

Knowing he couldn't die without telling Counter how he felt, he rose up on his elbows and looked Counter in the eye.

"Can you hear me?" Frink yelled.

Counter nodded, his eyes wide and wild with fear.

"I'm in love with you, Count," Frink yelled. "I've loved you for as long as I remember."

Counter's eyes went impossibly wider for an instant, his shock outweighing his fear. The shaft started to fill with dust, and Frink was having a tough time breathing and an even harder time talking, but somehow he had to find a way. He'd be damned if he'd leave this world without ever telling Counter. "I can't die without telling you...." Frink coughed to clear the dust from his burning throat. "I should have told you before."

Frink closed his eyes and kissed Counter gently on the lips. He saw a quick burst of light. *Wow, you really do see fireworks.* Then he felt something warm running down his head and neck. Suddenly, the rumbling started to subside, and it began to grow quiet. Then, complete silence. Frink was looking down, and he saw blood on Counter's face. *Counter, oh, God, Counter's hurt!*

Frink panicked. "Counter! Counter! Oh, my God, Counter, you're bleeding." Frink tried to stand, but he suddenly felt weak and collapsed. *Save Counter! What's wrong with me, I've got to save Counter.* Frink tried as hard as he could to move, but it was no use. Everything went black.

AS THE dust settled, Hepp and Counter searched for the opening to the tunnel. They went in opposite directions, each following the walls of

The Mystery of Ruby Lode

the shafts, and when they met at the other end, Counter yelled, "Hepp, that means we're trapped. We're trapped, Hepp."

"It's a good thing we're trapped 'cause if we ever get out of here, I'll kill ya."

"What are you talking about? What did I do to you?"

"You ain't done nothin' to me, but you sure as shit hurt that boy in there. He's done nothin' but love you, and he was man enough to tell you he loved you, and what do you do? You bash his head in with a rock."

"Damn sodomite. He's lyin', Hepp. I ain't had no relations with him."

"I don't believe ya, boy, but we've got bigger fish to fry right now."

Desperate to find a way out of the collapsed tunnel, Hepp started swinging his pick in the area where he thought the opening of the shaft was located. Counter followed his lead, and together but not speaking, they dug for eight hours with no end in sight. They moved to another location and repeated the process. The air was becoming heavier with each swing of the pick, but they kept at it.

WHEN Frink came to and opened his eyes, he was propped up against the wall of the shaft, and Shull was kneeling next to him.

"Counter?" was the first thing he mumbled. "Where's Counter? I need to save Counter."

He vaguely heard Shull's voice, but he couldn't make out what he was saying. Frink tried to move, to stand, and Shull pushed him back down.

"I've got to save Counter. Where's Counter?"

He felt a warm hand on his arm. He tried to focus, but everything was a blur. *Please help me find him. He's hurt and he needs me. God, please let me help Counter.*

"Frink! Snap out of it," Shull ordered.

"Shull," Frink whispered. "Counter? Is he okay?"

"Counter's all right," Shull assured him. "He's helping Hepp see if we can get out of here."

He's all right.

Frink took a deep breath. The fog in his head was starting to clear. "But Count was bleeding. Are you sure he's okay?"

"He's fine, son. You're the one bleeding."

"What? I saw blood on his face."

"Yeah, son, you saw blood on his face, but it was your blood, not his. You were hit with a rock while you were lying on top of him, protecting him."

Sudden relief filled Frink's senses. "He's okay?"

"Yeah, son, he's okay."

"I told him, Shull, did you hear me? I told him."

"I heard you, son," Shull said with a disappointed look on his face.

"Why the look, Shull? Aren't you proud of me for telling him?"

"I'm awful proud of you, son, but, Frink, Counter might need some time to digest the information, that's all. Don't expect too much too soon."

"Did he say anything? Was he worried about me?"

"I think between the collapse of the mine and your admission, he didn't seem none too happy."

"He'll be fine once we get out of here, Shull. I just know it."

"All right, son, just quiet down. You took quite a blow to the head," Shull warned. "Let me go check on the boys. I'll be right back."

Frink watched as Shull disappeared into the larger shaft. He was filled with anticipation. *I did it. I told him. Counter knows I love him.*

A few minutes passed and Shull returned with Hepp. "Is everything okay? Where's Counter?"

The Mystery of Ruby Lode

Shull looked at Hepp. "Everything's okay. He just needs a few minutes."

"A few minutes? A few minutes for what?" Frink asked.

"He's upset is all," Hepp reassured him. "He'll be fine."

Just then Counter came running into the shaft. "Is he awake?" He sneered. "Let me at 'im. Next time, I'll use a pick instead of a rock."

"Counter!" Frink exclaimed. "You're okay, thank God."

"What's it to ya, you damn sodomite?" Counter snickered.

"Count, what's wrong? What do you mean 'next time you'll use a pick'?" Frink asked.

Shull patted Frink on the arm. "Calm down, son. We've got to focus on trying to get out of here."

"Are we trapped?" Frink asked.

"The entrance to the main chamber is completely blocked off," Hepp confessed.

Frink's heart sank and all the blood drained out of his face. "What do we do now?"

"We pray," Shull said. "No one knows we're up here, so no one's going to be looking for us."

Frink got to his knees. "This can't be the end." *Oh God!* He grabbed his head when he felt a stab of pain. "That blasted rock really did a number on me."

"And the next time you try one of your sodomite moves on me, I won't just wound you, I'll kill ya, I will."

Frink's gut twisted painfully with Counter's admission, and he slumped back against the wall. "You did this to me?" he asked. *Please say no.* Bile rose up into his throat and he fought to keep it down. *God! Please don't tell me you did this.*

"Damn straight, you blasted queer. And as I said, touch me again and I'll kill ya."

"You ain't killin' nobody, boy," Hepp said as he stood guard over Frink with a pick.

Suddenly, it all made sense to Frink. His love confession had had the exact response he'd feared. *My life's over.*

Frink closed his eyes and said, "Go ahead and kill me. I'm dead anyway."

Shull put his arm around Frink and tried to comfort him.

"Get out of this shaft," Hepp told Counter as he and Shull surrounded Frink. "It's your damn fault we're in this situation anyway, yelling and kicking in an unstable mine. You put us here, son, so now you can see how it feels to die alone. Now git."

"I wouldn't stay with you anyway 'cause you're going straight to hell," Counter yelled as he kicked the side of the mineshaft again.

Tears were now forming in the back of Frink's eyes, but he was determined not to let Counter see him cry. "Just go, Count. It's over either way."

"Damn you, Frink. You were my best friend, and now you turn out to be a blasted queer."

"Count, if you think I'm a queer, then that makes you one too, because it takes two to do what we did last night."

Frink saw Counter's face get blood red. "We ain't did nothing, unless you took advantage of me while I was sleeping."

"Someone sleeping don't give me a hand job and then climb on top of me, shove their prick up my shitter, and shoot their load down deep in my gut."

"You're lyin', Frink. Stop lyin'."

"I'm not lyin' and you know it," Frink growled. "For the last twelve years, we did stuff night after night, and you expected me to believe that you were asleep every time and didn't know what you were doin'? You're only foolin' yourself, Count." Frink shook his head. "You're a bigger coward than I am."

"Why, I'll kill you, ya little fucker," Counter roared and took a step toward Frink.

Hepp stood up with the pick in his hand. "And I'll kill you if you lay one hand on him."

The Mystery of Ruby Lode

The air was now thick, and it was becoming harder and harder to breathe.

"Fine. Burn in hell, sodomites," Counter said as he turned and stormed out of the shaft.

Frink could no longer hold back the tears, and he began to sob. Shull held him close, and Hepp sat down on the other side of Shull and tried to comfort him as much as possible.

"We don't have much time. The air's 'bout gone," Hepp told Shull and Frink.

For the next few minutes, Frink tried not to eavesdrop as Hepp and Shull exchanged achingly tender words, their heartfelt good-byes to each other. But no matter how hard he tried, he hung on their every word. Their love was pure and strong, and Frink envied what they had. Even in death, they were together—arm in arm, heart-to-heart, content and grateful to have it that way when the end came.

Still, Frink longed to have Counter near him, to tell him how much he loved him and to hold on to until the end came. But Counter had made it perfectly clear how he felt about him. Even with death looming over his head, Count still couldn't admit there was ever anything between them, and that was the darkest day of Frink's insignificant and uneventful life. He knew he was dying physically, but it didn't matter because he was already emotionally dead inside. Counter had seen to that. At least he wouldn't have to worry about going on without Counter. That had already been decided when the mine collapsed, but he still couldn't stop his heart from breaking further at the thought of Counter being alone in the other shaft slowly dying, just as he was. No matter how hard he tried not to think of him, his efforts were in vain. Frink fished the deed to the mine out of his back pocket, reached in the bottom of his tool bag, and dug out a worn-down pencil. He turned the deed over and started writing. When he finished, he folded the deed and held it tightly in his hand.

As Frink fought to inhale each minuscule breath of air, he prayed for death to come quickly. He wanted to be released and free from his own emotional prison. His only consolation was in death the pain would end. Not the physical pain—he didn't give a damn about the physical pain—but the emotional pain. Pain so severe, he likened it to having his heart ripped out of his chest, sliced into little pieces, and squeezed until every last drop of the love he'd felt for Counter had disappeared into the dirt floor below. *Please let this be over soon.* And when the end did come, he wouldn't have to think about Counter ever again. That thought gave him as much peace as he would get as the end drew near.

The remaining air was disappearing quickly, and Frink fought every instinct to gasp for what little was left in the small shaft. It took everything he had to stay calm when every cell in his body was telling him now was the time to panic. As he closed his eyes for the last time, he felt Shull take his hand, and he was grateful for the touch and the feeling of not dying alone. Frink saw little stars starting to sparkle behind his eyelids, and suddenly his muscles started to tense. Just before he lost consciousness, his last thought was of Counter, dying alone. As the darkness began to take him, he took one final breath and whispered silently, "I love you, Counter."

Part TWO

NEW YORK CITY, NEW YORK
SPRING 2011

Chapter THREE

Cyrus Curran, Cy to everyone who mattered to him, sat at the foot of his bed and loosened and removed the tie from around his neck. He stretched and yawned as he slipped out of his black, highly polished Ferragamo loafers. Instinctively, he wiggled his toes, and the sight of his navy blue socks, with the gold threaded toes moving back and forth, quickly brought him back to Biloxi, Mississippi, when he was just six years old.

"Just get to the car," the young Cyrus told himself as he genuflected, made the sign of the cross, and bolted down the aisle of the Catholic Church. He vaguely heard his mother's orders to slow down, but he couldn't stop. When he finally reached the doors at the end of the longest aisle he'd ever seen, he took the steps two at a time down to the parking lot. He'd been so uneasy ever since his mother had dressed him for Sunday morning services, and now he was having a hard time catching his breath. As he ran, he pulled his arms out of his little suit coat, hoping less clothes might help him breathe easier, but it was no use. He got to the car and frantically pulled on the door, panicking for a second when he thought his daddy might have locked it. Just as he thought he might scream, the door opened and he jumped in and locked the door behind him. While fighting for air, he desperately fumbled with the shoestrings of his black church shoes, his hands shaking uncontrollably. "I've got to get these shoes off." The harder he tried, the more knotted the shoe laces became and the more panicked he felt.

He finally gave up on the laces and used every bit of strength he could muster to pull the shoes off without unlacing them. He took a deep breath when both shoes finally fell to the floor of the car with a thump and his toes were free to wiggle and move freely. He leaned his head back on the seat and closed his eyes. *How lame is it to be afraid of a pair of shoes?* he thought as his breathing began to even out and his hands stopped shaking. Eventually, his parents made their way to the car, and when they saw him in the back seat with no coat or shoes on, they pretended not to notice, but he'd seen the sad look on their faces.

W HEN the memory faded, Cyrus was still wiggling his toes, happy to be out of his shoes. To this day, he still couldn't imagine why, as a kid, he'd always felt so terrified and constricted when Sundays came around and his mother forced him wear his dress shoes to church. He especially remembered being frightened of his shoelaces, and even now, as an adult, none of it made any sense to him. Oddly enough, he still didn't own a pair of shoes that required shoelaces, but luckily, he was no longer afraid of them. He simply didn't like the feeling of being restricted or confined in any way, something else he'd brushed off as one of the many mysteries surrounding his life.

He'd also discovered much later in life that his family had abruptly moved from Long Island to Biloxi, supposedly because his father's job had been transferred, but the odd thing was, he didn't remember a time when he didn't live in Mississippi. He should have some recollection of living in another place. In addition, no one ever

The Mystery of Ruby Lode

talked about living on Long Island. *Why am I thinking about all of this again now?* He rolled his eyes before he closed them, lying back on the bed just for a second.

He was exhausted; the last two weeks on Wall Street had been a real nightmare. The stock market had been especially volatile, his investors were nervous, and the looming recession was front and center in everyone's mind. He sighed and pictured his approaching escape, a week in beautiful Colorado with the man he loved and his two best friends, all doing what they loved to do: exploring abandoned gold mines.

He chuckled when he thought about his hobby choice. He hated confined spaces or being restricted, but he loved exploring abandoned gold mines. What was up with that? In reality, most of the forsaken mines they'd explored were not confining in the least, and he knew he could leave anytime he wanted to. That made all the difference to him.

In the early planning stages of the upcoming trip, the group had begun searching Colorado's over five thousand abandoned mines, looking for anything odd that might jump out at them, and the hands-down winner was Ruby Lode. Cy had been intrigued by Ruby Lode because the last record on file regarding the mine was a tax lien sale in 1914 to four men named Frink Davis, Counter Stephens, Hepp Thomas, and Shull Johnson. The mine consisted of three shafts, two hand dug between 1906 and 1914—he assumed by the original owners—and the third dug almost one hundred years later by a prospector who didn't realize the mine was still deeded property. In addition, there was no record of the mine ever being worked. And the most exciting part of their research was that, according to the Bureau of Land Management, only one group had applied for a permit to explore the mine. That had been some ten years back, and after the first day, the permit was surrendered under strange circumstances with no data on any findings. Cy assumed the mine was just too small a blip on the radar for anyone to be concerned with. Anyone but them, of course.

He then searched further through census records for any information on the four owners and had turned up nothing on Counter

Stephens or Frink Davis. However, the census did show that, in 1904, Hepp Thomas and Shull Johnson purchased a piece of property in Lyons, Colorado, which, according to Google Maps, was approximately seven miles from the opening of the mine. But later records showed nothing on either of them past 1914. In Cy's mind, that meant either they bought the mine and left town the very same year, which was unlikely, or they died shortly after they purchased it. Either way, this proved to be an interesting find and worth their efforts.

There were two other mines—Old Smuggler and Highland Placer—located in the area, and they were both in the early running but were quickly eliminated because they'd been explored recently and were well documented. They'd decided to request permits for them as well, and if they had time after Ruby Lode, they would investigate. Getting permits from the US Bureau of Land Management to explore Old Smuggler and Highland Placer was a piece of cake, but it had taken them nearly six months to get the permit to explore Ruby Lode, for several reasons. First, Ruby Lode was located on private property and still deeded as such, so the Bureau was forced to get permission from the owners before issuing the permit. Second, no one knew the condition of the mine or how safe it was to enter, so all four of them had to show proof of their extensive experience and sign release forms just to be considered. Third, they had to agree to alert the local authorities on a daily basis before they entered and vacated the mine. And lastly, they had to agree to do an extensive report outlining what they found and the overall condition of the mine.

Cy opened his eyes and quickly looked at his watch. *Five o'clock? Shit. I can't believe I dozed off for an hour.* He hopped out of bed and ran for the closet. *Bo will be home any minute, and I promised him I would start packing. Maybe if I open the suitcases and throw a few things in, it will at least look like I attempted to keep my promise.*

Bowen McAlister was his partner of almost ten years. He owned and operated Adventures Underground, a New York City-based company specializing in organizing vacations for adventure seekers looking for the thrills of underground exploration. His specialty was finding, exploring, and preserving the history of abandoned gold mines out west. In fact, this trip was a reconnaissance mission to determine if Ruby Lode could be upfitted to add to his list of offerings. In the beginning, Cy had thought it odd Bowen wanted to start a company like that based in New York City, where the only things underground were the sewer and the subway, but Bo had convinced him that so many New Yorkers who held high-powered, hectic jobs had the need to escape the hustle and bustle of the city and also had the means to actually do it. When he'd put it like that, it made perfect sense.

Cy and Bowen had met a decade ago when they were both attending NYU. Bowen was a junior and a couple of years older than Cyrus. They had an immediate attraction and a very short courtship before they fell madly in love. Shortly after they met, Cy had introduced Bowen to his two best friends: Duff Gentry, whom Cy was dating very casually when he'd met Bowen, and Lockhart Dawson, his college roommate and the life of every party. They, too, were very interested in Bowen's then passion and now livelihood. All three of them had taken to it immediately, and since then, the four guys had traveled out west, extensively scouting possible sites for future adventures. In the last three years, they'd explored three hundred out of the tens of thousands of mines in Utah, and they were moving on to Colorado.

Cy heard the door to their New York apartment open and close. He moved quickly as he threw a few more things into their suitcases. Within minutes Bowen was leaning against the doorjamb with his arms folded across his chest, smiling at him.

Cy's throat went dry and warmth began to settle in his groin. God, even after ten years the sight of Bo still made his heartbeat quicken and his dick swell. Bowen McAlister was a man's man. Despite the fact he'd been put up for adoption at birth, knew nothing about his birth parents, and had spent his entire life in the foster care system being shuffled from one home to another, he was the most well-adjusted, protective, and loving man Cy had ever met.

In the looks department, he was drop-dead gorgeous. Five feet eleven inches of hot, sexy man. His hair was dark brown, and he wore it in a buzz cut. Cy preferred he wear it a little longer, but he had to admit, he loved the way the short strands tickled his palms. Bowen always sported a thin, short mustache and goatee because he thought it made his pretty face look a bit more rugged, and Cy agreed. He had the cutest little birthmark on his cheek, which Bowen himself didn't really care for, but Cy loved it and often referred to it as his beauty mark. That always made Bowen snicker. He had the most striking deep-blue, need-you eyes, and if Cy looked into them for more than a couple of seconds, he could lose himself forever. Bowen's smile... well, his smile was what had sealed the deal. It was warm and, when it turned sly, powerful enough to curl Cy's toes. Each physical trait was a study in masculine beauty, but together? Holy shit, what a package.

"Hey, baby," Bowen said, still smiling. He walked over, grabbed Cy by the back of the neck, and pulled him into a long, passionate kiss. Cy never tired of the way Bo took him and made him feel weak in the knees. When the kiss ended, Bowen looked into the suitcases and back at Cy. "Fall asleep, did ya?"

Cy smiled sheepishly. "Is it that obvious? I'm really sorry, Bo. I just sat on the edge of the bed for a second and woke up an hour later."

"No worries, babe. I'll help," Bowen offered with a chuckle. "Plus, we have plenty of time."

Cy rummaged through the closet. "What time does our flight leave again?"

"Nine fifty-five, but the car service is picking us up at seven o'clock."

Cy threw underwear into the suitcase. "Have you talked to Duff or Lockey?"

"Yep, about an hour ago. The car is picking Duff up at six-thirty and Lockey at six forty-five."

Cy disappeared into the closet again to grab another handful of clothing and heard Bowen yell, "Did you remember to call the hotel to see if the gear showed up?"

The Mystery of Ruby Lode

"I did," Cy admitted proudly, sticking his head out of the closet door. "I talked to them this afternoon, and everything arrived as planned."

"I just hope it's in one piece."

"You worry too much, babe. It'll be fine."

"I sure hope so."

Together they finished packing; then Cy stripped and jumped into the shower. Out of the corner of his eye, through the tiny New York–sized, glass-enclosed shower, he watched as Bo stripped and leaned back on the sink to wait his turn. Bo always complained about having to go last, but Cy had known since the first night they were together that Bo enjoyed the show, and he'd made it his mission to never disappoint. *Show time!* Cy closed his sapphire-blue eyes, turned and dipped his long blond locks under the shower, and allowed the hot water to stream down his lengthy frame. His bulky, muscular build was holding up pretty well, and he used it to his advantage. He filled his hands with shampoo and allowed his elegant, sensual fingers to knead his scalp slowly as he washed his hair. When he was finished, he stood under the spray and allowed the soap to run down his length and disappear into the drain below. He slowly squeezed an ample amount of body wash over his narrow but muscular chest and lathered his tanned skin unhurriedly, massaging his entire body as he washed. He ran his lathered hands up and down his ass cheeks and parted them just enough to wash his tight opening, bending over ever so slightly to make sure Bo didn't miss a thing. *Now to bring it home.* He used both hands alternately to massage his ample dick and balls until he was on the verge of a full-blown erection.

Cy turned off the water, smiled at Bo, and stepped out of the shower. This had become a little game, private and only between them, since the very beginning of their relationship, and he cherished this time as much today as he had ten years ago.

Bowen handed Cy a bath sheet and dropped down to his knees in front of him. Bowen took him into his mouth and swallowed him all the way down in one gulp. Cy closed his eyes and threw his head back, enjoying the sensation of Bo's warm lips sliding up and down his dick with just the right amount of friction, teeth, and pressure. Bowen moved slowly but deliberately, pushing all of Cy's buttons simultaneously, something he'd become an expert at over the last nine-plus years. Cy rolled his head from side to side, moaning with pleasure as he felt that all-too-familiar feeling start to build deep in his gut. Bowen stuck his finger in his mouth alongside Cy's dick, wetting it adequately before pulling it out. Bo reached under his balls and gently massaged that tender patch of skin between his sack and his opening. As Cy started to tense with his impending orgasm, Bowen slipped his finger into Cy's opening and honed in on that proverbial spot. Goose bumps formed all over his body as Bowen thoroughly massaged his prostate. Cy became seriously weak in the knees, saw stars, and screamed in passion as he erupted, shooting spurt after spurt down Bowen's throat. Bowen brought him down from the rush by gently draining him dry while he gingerly slipped his finger from Cy's opening.

Cy smiled and, in his best Scarlett O'Hara accent, quoted a line from *Gone With the Wind:* "Oh, Mr. McAlister, you act just like a tonic on me."

Bowen stood, smiled, and gave him a nice, deep kiss before slapping him on the ass. "Now I need a cold shower."

Cy tasted a bit of himself when Bowen kissed him. *I need to eat more sweets.* "No man of mine will ever need a cold shower," he protested.

"I will today. We're going to be late, and if we are, we will never hear the end of it from the guys. Catch me later?"

"Oh, I'll catch you all right, and that's a promise."

AT 6:55 the buzzer sounded at their door. Cy walked up and pressed the intercom. "Yeah?"

"Get your asses down here," Lockhart Dawson yelled from the street. "We're gonna be late."

"Shut your whining. We're on our way down. And we have plenty of time." Cy released the intercom button. "Car's here, Bo."

Bo popped out of the bedroom looking hotter than shit. *The man just can't help it. He's hot and that's that.*

"If you're waiting on me, you're backing up," Bo teased. "Did you check us in and print our boarding passes?"

"Check," Cy replied.

"Hotel and rental car confirmations?"

"Check."

"Permits?"

"Check."

"iPad?"

"Check."

"Luggage?"

"At the door."

"Okay then, Mr. Curran, I guess we're all set. Let's get this show on the road."

Cyrus threw his backpack over his shoulder, grabbed his roller board, and out the door he went with Bowen right behind him.

When the elevator reached the lobby and the doors opened, Cy saw Lockhart was waiting with his arms crossed over his chest, tapping his foot, wearing the tightest T-shirt Cy had ever seen. "What took you ladies so long?" he demanded.

Cy huffed. "Oh, shut up and get your pansy ass in the car."

Lockhart turned in an overly animated gesture and strutted toward the waiting car. Cy looked at Bowen and smiled at the antics of his friend.

Lockhart was the youngest of the group at twenty-seven years old. He'd been smart enough to skip a grade in high school, which made him a freshman at NYU at the ripe old age of seventeen.

Underneath the outgoing and well-liked party animal, he was damned smart and the only one of them to graduate with honors. He'd majored in marketing and right after graduation was recruited by one of the largest and most successful advertising agencies on Madison Avenue. On the surface, he was the epitome of a stereotypical gay man. He went to the gym almost daily, which resulted in a perfect set of highly toned abs tight enough to bounce a quarter off of, a well-developed chest, and very muscular arms and legs. His chocolate-brown hair, kept short on the sides but long on top, was always perfectly messed up as it topped off his six-foot frame. And when Lockhart smiled that million-dollar smile, look out: his dark-brown eyes sparkled with something no human could deny. He was the type of guy every gay man wanted in his bed, every straight man wanted as his best friend, and every woman drooled over. No mortal was immune to the charms of Lockey Dawson and, boy, did he know it.

But Cy had always known there was much more to Lockhart than met the eye. Although he'd never confirmed it, Cy felt certain under that love 'em and leave 'em party-boy exterior, Lockey had a special soft spot for one Duff Gentry.

THEY'D all stayed very close during and after college, traveled together extensively, and were very comfortable around one another. Cy threw his bags in the back of the sedan and peered into the window at his motley crew. "Here we go again, boys. Let the fun begin."

"Shotgun," Duff yelled as he climbed out of the backseat and hopped in the front, while Bowen, Cy, and Lockey took the back.

The ride to the airport was filled with the usual banter between Bowen and Lockey. But Duff, the shy one of the group, who normally tried to get a word in as often as he could, was fairly quiet.

While Bowen and Lockey reminisced about their last trip and argued over something no one really cared about, Cy leaned up to the front seat and put his hand on Duff's shoulder.

The Mystery of Ruby Lode

"You okay, buddy? You seem a little preoccupied."

"I don't know, Cy. I'm feeling a little uneasy about this trip."

DUFF had always been the one who seemed to have a sixth sense. In fact, he was downright psychic, and they all dealt with it wherever they went. They might be in the middle of dinner and Duff would start talking to the empty space beside him, or they might be walking down the street and he would have to stop someone and tell them "your late Uncle Harry says the money's in the coffee can buried in the back yard." He regularly saw dead people who were trapped on Earth, not realizing they were dead and needing to cross over. Some spirits were lost somewhere between this plane and the next. He also had premonitions—sometimes when good things were going to happen, but mostly when terrible things were brewing. At first it had freaked them all out, but they were so used to it now, it had become a given. In fact, it made exploring abandoned mines a little safer because he could sense if they were in danger.

He'd inherited his gift from his mother, who'd died when he was just six years old. She'd begun to work with him to develop his clairvoyance as soon as he could speak, but Duff's young life drastically changed when his mother died in childbirth, along with his baby sister. Not only did he lose the only stability in his life, but he'd lost the encouragement he needed to hone his craft. His father, not believing in their ability, forbade any further discussions about the "psychic crap," and that was that.

When Duff was eight, his father married a widow with four teenage boys of her own, and Duff's life again took a drastic turn for the worse when he simply got lost in the mix. His new family moved into his childhood home, and everyone seemed to have someone. His father had his new wife, and his stepbrothers had their mother, but Duff felt like he didn't have anyone. He was then forced to share a bedroom with his fourteen-year-old stepbrother, who was none too happy about the arrangement and didn't mind showing it every time he had the chance. He felt like an outsider in his own home, and he just wanted to fade away from everything and everyone. During that time, he realized when he was quiet or out of sight and didn't ask for anything, he was mostly left alone. Self-preservation took over and he became invisible, keeping completely to himself, which resulted in his growing shyness.

As he matured, he worked at overcoming his reticence and made a conscious effort to be a little more outgoing, but if truth be told, under it all he was still that painfully shy little boy trying to find a place to fit in.

However, where looks were concerned, Duff was every bit as handsome as Lockey. The difference being, where Lockey knew he was gorgeous and used it to his advantage, Duff didn't have a clue as to just how appealing he was or the effect his sweet, calm demeanor had on everyone around him. He was a little over six two and his hair was cut much the same way as Lockey's, but it was much blonder. Where Lockey's eyes were dark brown, Duff's lazy, bedroom eyes were hazel and were more deep set. He sported a full set of pouty lips, causing him to be called "trout mouth" all through college and teased mercilessly over the years about having them enhanced. But that just wasn't Duff, and everyone knew it. He was every bit as muscular as Lockey, but not from going to the gym. His muscles came from damn good genes. But again, he was as modest as they come. When he'd majored in broadcasting, everyone just assumed he would be in front of the camera, but being the shy Duff he was, he chose to work behind the camera. Right after graduation, he'd started out as a page at ABC and was now a segment producer for the *Good Morning America* show.

Duff and Cy had met on the first day of college, and although it took him a week to get up the nerve to ask Cy out, to his surprise Cy'd accepted and they'd dated a few times. That is, until Cy met Bowen, and that was the end of that.

"OKAY, Duff, can you be a little more specific? Like, is it our driver? No offense," he said to the driver while patting him on the shoulder.

The Mystery of Ruby Lode

"The flight, maybe, or the expedition? Give me something to go on here."

"It doesn't quite feel like the driver."

The driver looked away from the road just long enough to smirk at Cy.

"And it doesn't feel like the flight," Duff offered up, "which only leaves the expedition. Let me noodle on it some more."

"Oooo-kay," Cy said as he slid back on his seat, right into the middle of the same banter he'd escaped earlier.

"Hey, guys, Sylvia Browne up here is having another psychic moment. Can we give her a little quiet?"

Duff snapped his head around and glared at Cy.

"Duff, are you okay?" Bowen asked.

"Just give me a little while, will ya?"

Thirty-five minutes later, the car pulled into the loading and unloading zone at the LaGuardia terminal, and they all quickly jumped out. When the bags were unloaded, Cy tipped the driver and they headed into the terminal.

"So you're sure it's not the flight?" Lockey asked. "You know how I feel about flying."

Duff waved him off. "Nah, it's not the flight, Lockey. Relax."

Lockey smiled. "Well, then, what are we waiting for?"

Since they'd checked in online and already printed their boarding passes, they went straight to security. After waiting fifteen minutes just to get up to the conveyor belt, they took off their shoes and belts, emptied their pockets, removed their wristwatches and cell phones, took out their laptops, and plopped their roller boards onto the conveyor belt before standing in line for the body scanner.

"You guys better go first," Lockey warned. "'Cause when that guy sees my package, he's gonna be in awe and will most certainly want to stare at it for a while."

"Jeez, Lockey, that's funny, 'cause we've all seen your package and it has the opposite effect on us," Bowen joked.

"Go ahead, make fun, but this baby could stop a ship."

"Sink a ship is more like," Cy added. "Can we just go already?"

They all made it through security without incident, except Lockey, who had his lube confiscated for being over the three-ounce limit. He vowed to buy another bottle once they touched down in Denver. They re-dressed on the other side of the security checkpoint, and by the time they reached their departure gate, they still had fifteen minutes until it was time to board. Luckily, there was a bar directly across from the gate, so they headed over for a drink to start their vacation off right.

Duff was still unusually quiet. "Any signals from the great beyond, Sylvia?" Cy teased.

"Stop calling me that, asshole," Duff protested.

Cy frowned. "Come on, Duff, I call you that all the time. You must really be worried about something."

"Sorry." Duff rubbed his temples. "I just can't shake this feeling. Maybe I'm just tired."

"Get some rest on the plane and maybe you'll feel better when we land in Denver," Cy suggested. "Besides, once we land it's only thirty miles to Boulder, so it shouldn't take us more than forty-five minutes or so to get to the inn."

"Good idea," Duff agreed.

Minutes later, the gate attendant was calling for the boarding process to begin, so they paid the tab and hauled it over to the gate. Cy and Bowen settled in the bulkhead while Duff and Lockey were seated right behind them. Lockey flirted continuously with the first-class male flight attendant, or as he referred to him, the "air mattress," until they all had ample drinks and snacks. The plane pushed away from the gate on time and the four-hour flight began. While Bowen tried to nap, Cy kept looking around to check on Duff. He had to admit he was just a bit concerned about Duff's uneasy feeling.

"I'm a bit worried about Duff," Cy leaned over and whispered to Bowen, who was just dozing off.

The Mystery of Ruby Lode

Bowen opened his tired eyes. "He'll be fine. Maybe he's just tired, like he said."

"Duff wouldn't blow smoke up our asses if he didn't have a real concern."

"Let's just see how he feels when we land."

Duff slept most of the flight while Lockey, on the other hand, spent his time in the galley making plans with the "air mattress" for a layover, so to speak. They were all alerted when the three chimes indicated it was almost time to land. The flight attendant came over the loud speaker, but not before a giggle escaped his lips, to tell everyone to return all seatbacks and tray tables to their upright and locked positions. Cy watched as Lockey made his way down the aisle but stopped and winked at him before continuing on to his seat.

They landed shortly afterward, about thirty minutes ahead of schedule, and within an hour, they had picked up the rental car and were on the road to Boulder, minus one Lockhart Dawson, who had a date at the airport Marriott. Before they parted ways, Lockey swore he would be back at the inn before morning.

Bowen drove while Cy plugged the address into the GPS for the Alps Boulder Canyon Inn. GPS calculated forty-two minutes until their destination.

Cy turned to the back seat. "How're you feeling, Duff, any better?"

"Not really. I just can't shake this stupid feeling something bad is coming."

"Do you want to call off the expedition?" Bowen asked with concern.

"No! I mean... hell, I don't know," Duff admitted with a shrug. "If I say 'no' and something bad happens, I'll never forgive myself, and if I say 'yes,' then I may be ruining our vacation for no good reason."

"Duff, you know we're very careful at what we do and if we didn't have excellent track records, we wouldn't have had a chance at getting that permit," Cy reassured him.

"Logically, I know that, Cy. It's not about us being careful; it's about things that are out of our control. I need time to sort through all of this," Duff concluded. "I'll give you a report in the morning, and then when Lockey's back, we can all decide how to proceed."

Cy looked at his partner, and Bowen nodded at Cy's questioning gaze. "Fair enough."

They checked into their rooms, Cy and Bowen in one room and Duff and Lockey in the adjoining room. They unpacked while chatting through the open door until Duff finally appeared in the door in his boxers and a T-shirt. "I'm gonna turn in."

"You okay?" Bowen asked.

"Yeah. Still uneasy, but maybe I can sort through all of this in my dreams."

"Night, Duff," Cy called in a muffled tone, obviously brushing his teeth.

"Good night, guys. We'll talk in the morning."

DUFF sat bolt upright in bed. "Cyrus, no," he whispered. He was shivering, and his heart was beating a mile a minute. He instinctually wrapped his arms around himself to try and warm his chilled skin and realized he was soaking wet. *Where the hell am I?*

He did his best to focus on his surroundings, trying to find anything that would clue him in. He opened and closed his eyes several times, but nothing would come into focus. He finally reached over and turned on the light. An image of himself, white as a sheet with beads of sweat on his forehead and nose, stared back at him from the mirror of an unfamiliar dresser. Glancing from side to side, he saw an armoire, two club chairs, and an extra bed.

A hotel room. I'm in a hotel room. Right. Colorado. Ruby Lode.

Peeling the covers back, Duff put his feet on the floor and sat on the side of the bed. He held his head in his hands and willed himself to calm down. When he thought his shaking legs were steady enough to

The Mystery of Ruby Lode

hold him, he went to the bathroom, drew a glass of water from the faucet, and took a long drink. He cupped his hands under the faucet and splashed cool water on his face then blindly fumbled until he recognized the touch of a terry cloth hand towel. He dried his face and hands, but when he opened his eyes and looked into the mirror, it was not his reflection he saw, but the reflection of someone he didn't recognize. Startled at first, but not completely unused to this sort of thing, he froze and tried to focus on the face.

He blinked his eyes again. "Who the hell are you?"

But in a flash, the stranger's face disappeared and his own confused reflection was staring back at him.

What in the hell?

He got back into bed, rested against the headboard, pulled his knees up to his chest, and tried to determine what had just happened. *I was having a nightmare, but what was it about?* Resting his chin on his kneecaps, he tried to remember details.

Cy was in it. We were in a dark, damp place, a mine, probably, and we were sitting on the ground leaning against a wall.

Then little bits and pieces started to flow back into his mind.

Oh, my God! Cy was gently rubbing my leg, and then he suddenly kissed me.

"Why is that so bad?" he whispered to himself with a certain amount of shame. "I've been dreaming about that happening for the last ten years." He started remembering more of the dream.

He urged me onto my back, and I closed my eyes. He lay on top of me and kissed my face and neck.

As the memory came back, he immediately started to feel guilty and embarrassed, but the guilt alone couldn't stop the erection already forming in his shorts.

We were passionately making out, and his hands were all over me. He was rubbing my groin, but when I opened my eyes, it was no longer Cy on top of me.

A chill ran down Duff's spine when he recognized the man in his nightmare as the same man he'd just seen in the reflection of the mirror. The memories were coming faster and faster now, and his heart was increasing at the same pace.

My arms were pinned over my head and my blue jeans were being ripped off. My knees were suddenly forced against my chest. The stranger smiled an evil smile and rammed his way in. Pain!

Tears were now streaming down his face, and his body trembled as he remembered the violation to his body. *Calm down, Duff. It was just a dream, just a dream.* It seemed so real, more than just a nightmare, as if the entity or spirit was trying to scare him, but why? *Why would he want to rape me? But he first appeared as Cyrus. Always Cyrus. Oh, my God, Cyrus, this can't go on. When in the hell am I going to be over you? You would think ten years of being around you while you are in love with someone else would snap me out of this stupid fantasy. I can't keep doing this any longer. What in the hell am I going to do?*

Duff heard a key in the door, and for a split-second, fear overtook him. The door opened, and he heard Lockey's soft voice. "What are you doing awake at this hour?"

When Duff turned his tear-streaked face to meet Lockey's, he saw his friend's questioning expression turn to one of concern. In seconds, Lockey was at his side with his arms open. Duff fell into them without hesitation. He began to sob, and Lockey gently stroked his back and allowed him to get it out of his system. When he shed his last tear, he pushed away from Lockey and wiped his eyes.

Lockey looked at him with so much concern. "Are you ready to tell me what this is all about?"

Duff pulled two tissues from the box on his bedside table and blew his nose. "I don't know where to start."

Lockey smiled. "How about at the beginning?"

"How much time do we have?"

The Mystery of Ruby Lode

Lockey pulled off his boots and climbed into bed next to Duff. "All night, if need be."

Duff hesitated. *I've got to tell someone, but can I trust him to keep my secret?*

"Why are you being so nice to me?" Duff teased.

"Come on, I'm not as big an asshole as everyone makes me out to be." Lockey must have seen the tug of war going on in his head. "Look, buddy, whatever it is that's eating away at you, you can tell me. You know that, right?"

Duff nodded and sighed. "It's Cy," Duff whispered.

"What about Cy?"

Duff hesitated again. He'd never told a soul how he felt about Cy. But now it seemed if he was going to keep his sanity, he needed to take a chance. Duff took a deep breath. "You remember that Cy and I were casually dating when he met Bowen, right?"

"Yeah, I remember."

"Well, ah… I, ah…."

"You still have a thing for the guy."

Duff suddenly felt himself flush. "You know?"

"Jesus, Duff, I suspected, but…."

"What do you mean, you suspected?"

"You keep it hidden very well, but every once in a while, when you think no one is looking, I catch you staring at him. And there's just something in the way you look at him that made me want someone to look at me that way. I just felt like there was something more to it."

Duff panicked again. "Oh, God, Lockey, I hope Bowen's never picked up on anything."

"It wouldn't matter. Bo and Cy are solid as a rock, and knowing Bowen, he'd take it as a compliment. I mean you've never thrown yourself at Cy, you've never made it obvious, and you've never disrespected Bowen in any way, so why would he be upset?"

"I don't know. I just feel like I've been deceitful and not being honest with either of them."

"Look, Duff, I don't tell you all my secrets, so why should you 'fess up to all of yours? Just because we're best friends, doesn't mean we have to tell each other everything."

"What do I do, Lockey? It's been ten fucking years, and I'm still pining away for someone I dated for—what… two weeks at best?"

"You've got to stop trying to deny it. You have to accept it, deal with it, and get past it. In addition, you've got to get out there and find someone else to fall in love with. When that happens, it will all be okay. There are lots of great guys out there."

"Is that why you're still single? No one dates more than you."

Lockey rolled his eyes. "I don't date, I sleep around, and there's a big difference. But I'm just biding my time, waiting for the one."

"But I'm not like you, Lockey. You walk into a room and everyone wants to know you, be around you, be with you."

"First of all, that's not true, but, boy, I sure wish it were."

Duff patted his knee. "Oh, it's true all right, and I have tons of proof."

"Regardless, Duff, you have me in the looks department hands down, and you're a great guy to boot. I'm just the life of the party. Do you know how exhausting that can be?"

"Stop it, Lockey, that's a load of crap. You're a hell of a lot more than just the life of the party."

"It's not crap at all. One of the greatest things about you is you don't realize how drop-dead gorgeous you are. You may not see how people react when you walk into a room, but I do."

"Now that's a load of crap."

"The hell it is. You're hot, Duff, and that shyness is such a big turn-on to guys. You just need to be open to it and love will find you. Sometimes it's staring you right in the face and you don't even see it."

"How do you do it, Lockey? When you walk into a room, the entire place lights up."

"I'm not sure about that, but I wasn't always the way I am now," Lockey said, climbing off of the bed, nervously standing and shoving his hands in his pockets.

Duff immediately missed Lockey's comforting touch and watched him closely as he appeared to be struggling with something.

"Look, I've never told anyone about this, but since you shared your little secret, I guess I owe you one."

"You don't owe me, Lockey," Duff protested.

Lockey pulled his hands out of his pockets and waved them through the air. "No, you're right. I don't owe you anything, but maybe I need to get this off of my chest."

Duff was suddenly concerned for his friend and patted the space next to him on the bed.

Lockey hesitantly sat down next to Duff again and took a deep breath. "When I was a kid, I was fat, dumpy, had a face full of acne, and I was bullied and teased mercilessly." Lockey's voice cracked. Duff reached over and put his hand on Lockey's knee and received a half-hearted smile in return.

Lockey covered Duff's hand with his own and continued. "The fact that my dad was in the Army and we moved sometimes twice a year didn't help. The first time I remember moving to a new Army base, I wasn't old enough to form any attachments to my friends, so moving didn't really affect me. But a couple of moves later, I'd just turned six years old and started first grade. Going to school every day, I was able to make a couple of friends, and it felt really good. I was starting to feel better about myself and everything was okay. Six months after that, like clockwork, it was time to move again, and it all turned horribly ugly when I had to leave my two best friends behind. It hurt a lot, but of course I survived. As I got older, each move made it harder and harder to make new friends, knowing I was just going to leave them when my dad got his orders to move again. So eventually, I just gave up and didn't bother to make any new ones. The pain just wasn't worth it."

"That sucks. I'm sorry, Lock."

Lockey smiled that halfhearted smile again and stood. He began pacing as he continued his story. "So in lieu of friends, I became idle and withdrawn and ate everything in sight. I started to put on weight, and of course puberty didn't make any of that any easier. What little self-esteem I had went right out of the door. But most importantly, I stopped connecting with people on any level."

Duff stood. "I have a hard time believing that, Lock. No one would ever believe, looking at you now, that you were that insecure kid."

"Yeah, well, maybe not, but that doesn't mean it isn't true," Lockey said, his voice cracking again.

Duff put his arms on Lockey's shoulders and looked him in the eyes. "But you're the most self-assured, outgoing person I know."

Lockey stepped away from the embrace and turned to look out of the window. "Because that's what I want people to see, but in the back of my mind, I'm still the insecure fat kid with terrible acne who had no friends."

Duff walked up behind him, put his arms around Lockey's waist, and laid his head on his shoulder. "I'm really sorry."

This time Lockey didn't pull away. "Don't be. For the most part I'm over it, except the connecting with people part. As I started dating, it was so hard for me to connect with people and trust them that eventually they just gave up on me and moved on. For me it was just one more thing to lose, so I learned if I left them before they could leave me, it didn't hurt near as much. And that's the Lockey you see today: Mr. Hit-and-Run."

"I'm not sure about the inability to connect with people. I feel like we're connecting right now."

Lockey turned within Duff's embrace, facing him and throwing his arms over Duff's shoulders. "Duff, I've known you for ten years, and I'd trust you with my life."

Duff smiled and gently reached up and brushed the tear from Lockey's cheek with his thumb. "So how do you do it?"

The Mystery of Ruby Lode

"Do what?" Lockey asked.

"Be the outgoing, studly man's man, when inside you're the fat insecure kid with no friends."

"The same way you wake up every day and pretend you're not in love with Cy, I guess. We do what we have to do."

Duff moved and again sat on the foot of the bed, patting the space next to him as an invitation. "When did you turn the corner and start to become the person you are today?"

Lockey sat on the bed next to Duff, rested his elbows on his knees, and thought a second before he spoke. "When I was sixteen, I think. We moved to a new Army base, and it had this incredible gym. Going to the gym was something I could do on my own and not have to interact with anyone, so it became my obsession. The more I worked out, the more weight I lost, and the bigger my body got. People started to notice me, and when I say 'noticed me,' I mean in a good way. Little by little, my self-esteem grew, and I crawled out of the dark place I'd been living in." Lockey clapped his hands and then stood. "But damn it, Duff, we're here to help you! Why do I always make things about me?"

"Stop it! You needed to get this out. Why can't we help each other?"

"I think I'm too far gone for help, but Duff, you're an incredible guy, and just for the record, anyone would be lucky to have you."

Duff punched Lockey in the shoulder. "Thanks, Lockey. But I think you're pretty damn incredible yourself."

Lockey laughed. "Now that we have that out of the way, we still haven't solved your problem. What do we do about you and Cy?"

"There is no me and Cy, and there's nothing to solve. You, Cy, and Bowen are my best friends, and I would never do anything to ruin that, nor would I do anything to come between Cy and Bowen. So the way I look at it, it's my problem, and I need to get over it. And believe me when I say, I've been trying for the last ten years, but maybe now that you know, you can help me. But Lockey, there's one more thing."

Lockey smiled that all-too-familiar smile. "You're not in love with me and Bowen too, are you?"

"Very funny. But no."

"I figured as much. Damn, I'm always a bridesmaid, never a bride."

Duff cocked his head to one side at the off-the-wall comment but brushed it off as a joke. "Get serious, Lock."

Lockey's smile quickly faded and he looked a little hurt.

Duff realized he must have sounded a little harsh. "Sorry, Lock. That came out wrong."

"That's okay," Lockey replied. "I get that all the time. So you were saying."

Duff didn't know how to respond to that, so he skipped right over it. "You remember I was having this uneasy feeling in the car on the way to the airport, right?"

"Yeah, I heard a thing or two about it in the car."

"Well, I had this nightmare…."

Duff nervously told Lockey about being raped in his nightmare and the face in the mirror.

"What do you make of it?" Lockey asked.

"I'm not sure, but you know most of my dreams are more like premonitions, and that in itself scares the hell out of me."

Duff felt a chill run down his spine and wrapped his arms tightly around himself to counteract the feeling. "I mean, Cy of all people. I know Cy would never rape me, but it wasn't really Cy. It was someone else in the end. Something or someone is trying to hurt me, and I don't know why."

"Come here," Lockey whispered as he pulled Duff into a hug. "I won't let anyone hurt you."

Duff returned the embrace and reveled in the security of Lockey's arms around him, protecting him. But he knew better than to count on anyone, because when it came down to it, he was alone and he knew it.

The Mystery of Ruby Lode

"Let's try and analyze your nightmare and focus on one thing at a time," Lockey suggested. "I think the most obvious place to start is with Cy."

Duff broke free from Lockey and started pacing back and forth in the small hotel room. "Lockey, there's nothing I can do about the way I feel about Cy. I've thought about this endlessly, and there's no sense telling him or Bowen because nothing is going to change where they are concerned. I just need to get over him, and maybe with your support, I can do that. It just helps to know I can talk to someone now. It was an awfully big burden to handle alone for all these years."

"You can count on me. I promise, I'll help anyway I can."

Duff crawled back into bed and pulled the covers up to his neck. "Now on to the bigger problem. First thing in the morning, we need to tell Cy and Bowen about the dream, minus the part about... Cy coming on to me."

"But I feel like the rape has relevance to the story."

"I guess you're right. I need to come up with another version of that part.... I know, can I say it was you who came on to me?" Duff asked rather shyly.

Lockey smiled. "Sure, I'll take one for the team."

"That tough, huh? And you wonder why I don't date."

"I'm teasing," Lockey confessed.

"Speaking of dates, how was the flight attendant?"

"Actually, he was very nice. Made me feel a little guilty about calling him an air mattress."

"I guess it's a stupid question to ask if you'll see him again."

Lockey grinned. "Yep, stupid question."

Duff smoothed the sheets and fluffed his pillow. "Okay then, we need to get some sleep. We have a big day tomorrow."

Lockey looked a little nervous as he stared at Duff. "You mind if I bunk in with you? No sense in unmaking a bed for a few hours."

Duff cocked his head and raised an eyebrow. "Nah, I don't mind, but you damn well better take a shower."

Lockey smiled proudly. "Already did that at the Marriott."

Duff laughed as he watched Lockey strip down to his boxer briefs and climb into bed, snuggling up behind him. Over the years, they'd bunked in many times, but something about tonight felt different. Suddenly, it felt good to have Lockey spooning him from behind. Why hadn't he noticed before how perfectly they fit? He felt one of Lockey's arms around his waist and then hesitant fingers lightly brushing his hair. Duff felt his face flush and blood started to rush to his groin. *Stop it, Duff, this is stupid. He's just being sweet because you told him about Cy and the nightmare.*

Chapter FOUR

THE next morning, they woke relatively early and headed down to breakfast. Again Cy noticed Duff was still very quiet, but the life of the party, always happy Lockey, was abnormally quiet as well. Usually the morning after a conquest, Lockey was full of details, whether anyone wanted to hear them or not.

The waitress filled their coffee cups, and they all enjoyed their first sips of java. Cy glanced at Bowen and then shifted his glance to Duff and Lockey on the other side of the booth. "How're you feeling this morning, Duff? Anything we should know about?" Cy asked.

Duff and Lockey exchanged glances, and Cy knew something was up.

"What gives, guys? What are you not telling us?"

Duff cleared his throat. "I had a pretty eventful evening."

"Well, good for you, Duff. You don't get out near enough," Cy teased.

Duff sighed. "Not that kind of eventful evening, you idiot."

Cy's face fell in an immediate frown. "Come on, Duff, lighten up."

"You won't tell me to lighten up after you hear what I have to say."

Bowen shifted, put his elbows on the table and rested his chin on top of his joined hands. "Uh-oh, I don't like the sound of that."

"Me either," Cy added.

Duff took another sip of his coffee and straightened in his seat. "I had a pretty bad nightmare, but I think it was much more than a nightmare. It was more like a premonition, and something was trying to make a point."

Cy raised an eyebrow and threw Bowen a nervous glance. "You've got our full attention now, buddy."

"I was raped in the nightmare."

"Raped," Cy echoed.

"Yes, but it didn't start out that way." Duff hesitated then felt Lockey's leg press against his under the table, he assumed as a show of support.

"Come on, Duff, spill it," Cy begged.

Duff relived the nightmare step-by-step to his friends, nervously replacing Cy with Lockey, and followed up with the incident in the bathroom and the whole "reflection in the mirror" thing.

Cy listened in silence, his entire body becoming more and more tense as the story unfolded. When Duff was finished, they were all silent.

"Most of your dreams and nightmares are premonitions, aren't they?" Cy asked, looking at Duff. "But rape?"

Cy was confused and a little angry. He turned his gaze to Lockey and then back to Duff. "Lockey would never rape you."

"Of course he wouldn't," Duff acknowledged.

"Thanks, Duff," Lockey said, smiling at Cy.

"Remember, in the nightmare, the rapist was not Lockey in the end; it was someone else, someone I don't know. And... all my dreams and nightmares aren't always premonitions. Some are just dreams."

Relaxing a little, Cy took a deep breath and reached out, covered Duff's hand with his own and squeezed.

Duff looked around the table at his friends and realized how lucky he was. "It's okay, boys, I deal with this all the time. Besides, that nightmare was the most action I've seen in a long time."

Everyone laughed. "But you and Lockey?" Cy said, trying to sound surprised. "Are you two doing the nasty and not telling us?"

"No!" Duff said while Lockey simply wiggled his eyebrows, which quickly earned him an elbow to the ribs.

Duff gave Lockey the evil eye. "You're not helping," he scolded.

"Sorry."

With a straight face, Cy asked, "Then how come Lockey was the one in the nightmare?"

"I don't think Lockey's part in this is as important as the rapist's part. I think the spirit or the entity, whatever it is, got into my head and used someone I care about to get to me."

"So you admit it," Cy said.

"Admit what?"

"Admit that you care for Lockey."

"Of course I care for Lockey. He's my friend." Duff paused and gave Cy a look that Cy knew all too well. "Cyrus, give it a rest," he continued. "I think your made-up love affair between Lockey and me is the least of our worries. Don't you?"

"Okay, okay, sorry."

Lockey noticed Bowen had remained quiet up to this point, obviously trying not to get in the middle of the banter, but he was starting to fidget. "So, Duff, what do you want to do about all of this?"

"That's just it, I don't know."

"Do you think this has something to do with the gold mine?" Bowen asked.

"I'm not sure yet. But so far I don't feel like we're in danger. The dream took place in what I think was a mine, but I didn't feel like my distress was caused by where I was, but more by who I was with."

Lockey attempted to interject a bit of humor and break the somber mood. "Of course you weren't in distress, you idiot. You were being loved by me—at least the enjoyable part, anyway."

Duff elbowed Lockey in the ribs yet again. "Come on, Lockey, I'm being serious."

"Stop elbowing me in the ribs!" Lockey protested, leaning against him. "That's going to leave a mark. And for the record, I am being serious. No one has ever been in distress while they were being loved by me."

Cy realized the old Lockey was finally rearing his ugly head, and he smiled broadly at his friend's antics.

"So what do we do?" Bowen asked.

"Let's do our reconnaissance trip to the mine today and see if I get anything when we get there. If not, we go down as planned."

"Duff, give it up, would ya?" Lockey teased again. "It was just a dream. No one's going down on anyone."

Duff slammed his hand down on the table. "Oh, good Lord, will you give it a rest?"

Bowen and Cy simply rolled their eyes at their weird choice in friends.

ANXIOUS to get their adventure started, they ate breakfast quickly and went back to their rooms to change clothes and get the gear, permit, and other paperwork. Their first day was going to be a reconnaissance mission to locate the opening of the mine and determine what equipment they would need to get down the mine's practically vertical shafts.

The Mystery of Ruby Lode

"You ladies ready to go?" Cy asked through the adjoining door.

"Who are you calling a lady?" Lockey asked. "My chance at being a lady escaped along with my hundredth trick."

Cy looked at Duff and smiled. "How're you feeling, buddy? Anything we should know about?"

"Nothing yet, but I'll let you know."

"Okay, boys," Bowen yelled from the other room. "Let's get a move on."

Lockey jumped to attention and saluted no one in particular. "Aye aye, Captain."

They got out to the rental Jeep and threw their equipment in the back. Bowen volunteered to drive and Cy called shotgun, so Lockey and Duff climbed in the backseat. Cy dug into his backpack and pulled out the location certificate. "Did you guys ever read this? It's pretty cool."

Lockey stuck his open hand between the seats. "I don't think I did."

Cy passed the document to Lockey and began searching in his backpack again.

"I don't think I saw it either," Duff admitted. "Read it out loud?"

"It's the official Location Certificate, dated January first, 1906.

"Know all Men by these Presents. That O.E. Jasper of the County of Boulder in the state of Colorado claim by right of discovery and location fifteen hundred feet linear and horizontal measurement on the Ruby Lode, along the vein thereof with all its dips variations and angles together with seventy five feet in width on each side of the middle of the vein at the surface; and all veins, lodes, ledges, deposits and surface ground within the lines of said claim eleven hundred and forty feet on said lode running north six degrees, twenty-three feet from the center of the discovery shaft and three hundred sixty feet running south six degrees, twenty-three feet west from said center of discovery shaft. Said claim is situated on the south side of the South St. Vrain Creek in the central mining district, County of Boulder and State of Colorado."

As Lockey read the document, Cy found the map he'd created on his laptop with Google's GPS application, showing the exact coordinates and directions to the mine's opening. He fed the information to Bowen to try and get them to the closest navigable road before they had to leave the Jeep behind. They knew from their extensive research the mine was very near the top of an almost vertical peak, and there were no roads that could get them anywhere near their target, so they would get as close as they could with the Jeep and hike the rest of the way. In addition, Cy had used Google Earth and printed visual confirmation, utilizing satellite images that clearly showed the mine's opening exactly where it was supposed to be.

When the Jeep finally reached the end of a long dirt road at the base of the mountain, they all climbed out and stretched their legs. Feeling the same nervousness and anticipation they always had just before they started an expedition, they began unloading the equipment and sorting through the various climbing and rappelling gear. Next they surveyed their surroundings and reviewed the map.

"It sure is beautiful here," Duff admitted. "Look how green the evergreens are against the bright blue of the sky."

Lockey looked up and then at the mountain range. "Breathtaking, and not a cloud in the sky. The terrain doesn't look too bad, at least what I can see from here."

Bowen followed his gaze. "A lot of big boulders, and the loose rocks might be a little tricky, but there's not much undergrowth, and that will help a lot."

"Ah, guys," Cy added pointing up the mountain. "Don't forget the mine's opening is at the tip top of that vertical peak. It'll be tough going the closer we get."

They all nodded in agreement as they began preparing for the climb by trading their sneakers and T-shirts, Cy's sneakers being slip-ons for obvious reasons, for Wellington climbing boots and long-sleeved shirts. They each harnessed up and put one set of lines over a shoulder and several others in each backpack.

The Mystery of Ruby Lode

On his iPad, Cy opened the Google GPS application that would help them navigate the large evergreens and rocky terrain to the mine's opening. They locked the Jeep and started up the mountainside with Bowen in the lead and Duff bringing up the rear. For the first hour, the hike wasn't too bad, but the closer they got to their destination, the more vertical the climb became. When they were about one hundred yards from the mine, the topography became almost completely vertical, and they were forced to use rocks and what little vegetation there was to steady themselves as they climbed. It took them almost the same amount of time to negotiate the last hundred yards as it did to get the majority of the way up the mountainside. Bowen was the first to make it to the mine, and the others watched as he secured a line to a large rock standing guard like a sentinel at the mine's opening. He threw the line down to help them climb up the last fifty feet.

WHILE the others made their way up, Bowen sat on the large rock and looked around at the hundred and eighty degree panoramic view. The late morning sun was reflecting off the snow-covered peaks of the distant Rocky Mountains as the evergreens danced against the deep-blue spring sky. The scene was so crisp and clear it looked like an oil painting. Bowen was feeling like he could almost reach out and touch the nearby mountains and sky when something caught his eye. He looked over his shoulder to the top of the peak behind him and did a double take. His stomach dipped and a dreadful chill ran down his spine. A young woman, holding what appeared to be an infant, was standing on the peak of the mountain wearing some type of uniform. It almost looked like a cheerleading uniform, but the old-fashioned type: black-and-gold, sleeveless all-in-one with a big *T* on the chest and a pleated skirt. He used his hands to shade his eyes from the glare of the sun and squinted and blinked several times as if he thought they were playing tricks on him, but every time his eyes opened, she was still there. To make things worse, she now looked to be losing her footing as unsteady rocks shifted under her feet. *What the hell? What was she doing up there with that baby?*

Instinct took over, and without thinking, he was on his feet attempting to make his way up to her before she dropped the baby, or even worse, they both fell to their deaths. He climbed over a boulder and lost sight of her for a split second, but when she came back to his view, she was holding the infant over her head like someone would do with a basketball right before they threw it across the court. "Stay there, I'm on my way to get you!" he yelled, not realizing what was about to happen. She smiled the most evil smile he'd ever seen and yelled down to him, "Take him! I never loved him, and I don't want him! He ruined my life!"

His heart began to race, and he broke into a sweat. He was scrambling to get to her before she did something she would surely regret. Now within ten feet of her, Bowen shuddered as he could clearly see the little baby being held overhead wrapped in a blue blanket. He stopped and looked up, hoping she saw the dread in his eyes as he pleaded with her in a soft, gentle voice. "It's okay, honey, just don't move. I'll be there in a flash and take you and the baby to safety. I promise everything will be fine."

Bowen took another step, but before he could get to her, she threw the baby over his head and down the mountainside. *Oh, my God! No!*

He watched it all play out in slow motion as the baby took flight, headed in his direction. He kept his eyes on the infant and jumped as high as he could to catch it, but the baby passed within inches of his fingertips. In a last ditch attempt, he turned and dove down the mountain, trying to intercept the baby before it made contact with the rocks below. His arms were stretched out in front of him and his hands were wide open as he sailed through the air. He was about to make contact with the baby when it disappeared in midair. And then he hit the ground. *Thump!*

He felt the air rush out of his lungs at the force of the impact, and then he began rolling down the mountain, trying to catch his breath.

The Mystery of Ruby Lode

Somewhere in the distance, he heard Cy's panicked voice calling his name. He rolled and tumbled; instinct took over and he tried to grab for anything that could help stop his fall. He felt a sharp pain as his head bounced off of a rock, but he pushed through the pain, trying to stop his body from barreling down the mountainside. Suddenly, he hit something that spun him a quarter of the way around, and he was now sliding feet-first on his stomach. He dug his Wellingtons into the dirt while using vegetation to slow his descent until he finally came to a stop at the base of a huge evergreen. He tried to stand but felt a stab of pain in his head and dizziness overtook him. He saw the earth quickly coming up to him as everything went black.

HE WAS free falling and spinning out of control. The cheerleader and the baby were always just inches out of his reach, and he was fighting the worst case of vertigo he'd ever experienced. His stomach churned, and he thought he might throw up. He wanted to stop the spinning and grab hold of the baby, but he was powerless against the free fall. He was just about to reach for the baby one last time when suddenly something was pulling him in the opposite direction. The cheerleader was gone and the baby was slipping farther and farther away from him. He struggled against the force, but he was too weak to keep it up. Defeated, weary, and brokenhearted, he gave up and let whatever was pulling him away take over.

SHEER will made Bowen open his eyes, but he quickly shut them against a bright light. He blinked several times through pools of tears in an attempt to bring something, anything, into focus. When he recognized Cy, who was holding and cradling him, he took a deep breath and tried to speak. "Cy, the baby. Did you get the baby?"

"Baby? What baby?" Cy asked.

Realizing now that they hadn't seen the baby, Bowen panicked and tried to move. "I need to get up. I need to find the baby."

Bowen felt strong arms holding him down and fought against them, but with no strength left, he was unable to move. His emotions got the best of him, and he began to cry.

"Bowen, listen to me!" Cy yelled in an attempt to reason with him. "You fell down the mountain and hit your head. Are you in pain? Can you move your arms and legs? Is anything broken?"

Bowen heard the words, but he couldn't focus on anything but the baby. "The baby?" He whimpered. "Cy, please help me find the baby."

He blinked again and through his tears, Duff and Lockey came into view.

"Guys, please help me," he asked a little more loudly.

"We're here, buddy! Are you in pain?" Duff asked.

Bowen shook his head from side to side. "I'm okay, but I've—got—to—find—the—baby," he said deliberately as he used every bit of energy he could find to try and get up.

Frustration overtook him as again he realized he was being held down. "Let me up!"

"Bowen, stop fighting us. There is no baby," Cy tried to explain. "You must have been dreaming while you were knocked out."

No baby? Bowen tried to think. The mountain, the cheerleader, the baby! Could it all have been a dream?

Becoming more aware of his surroundings and seeing Cy, Duff, and Lockey kneeling over him, he slowed his breathing and attempted to clear his head. When he spoke next, he wanted to sound like he was sane. "Didn't you see the girl… in the cheerleader uniform… at the top of the peak? She threw a baby off the mountain."

Emotion overtook him and he began to cry again as he relived the moments before the cheerleader threw the baby off the mountain. "How could someone throw a baby away?"

"Baby, you were dreaming," Cy tried to explain.

The Mystery of Ruby Lode

"No!" he screamed. "She was there, I know what I saw. When she threw the baby off of the mountain, I dove to try and catch it, but just before my hands were about to touch it, the baby disappeared."

Cy wiped Bowen's tears away. "Bo, there was no woman with a baby, and if there were, you said yourself the baby disappeared. If the baby disappeared, then it couldn't have been real, right?"

Bowen thought for a moment. *He's right. If it disappeared, how could it have been real?* He conceded and closed his eyes.

Cy was visibly shaken. "Jesus Christ, baby, you scared the shit out of us. You could have been killed. Let's get you down to the Jeep and to a hospital. I think you're gonna need a few stitches. Are you sure you're okay, no broken bones? Move your arms and legs for me."

Bowen did as he was told, and the guys saw everything seemed to be in working order.

Lockey put his hand on Cy's shoulder. "He'll be fine. Cy, he's just disoriented. It happens all the time with a blow to the head."

Bowen watched silently as Lockey ripped the sleeve off of his shirt and tied it around his head. "This will do until we can get you down the mountain."

Bowen regained his composure and was a little shaky as he attempted to sit up, still not believing what had just happened to him. Then, a few minutes later, the three of them helped him to his feet. Cy held him up as Duff and Lockey fastened the lines to the evergreen tree and secured him to Cy's harness. Feeling safe with his back against Cy's chest, he remembered just how much he loved this man. Without having to worry about his descent, Bowen had time to relive the entire incident. It had all happened so fast.

How could they have not seen the girl or the baby? They were just fifty feet below me. Could it have all been an illusion? No! I'm not crazy! I know what I saw.

They rappelled down the mountain with Cy controlling their descent until the terrain leveled out enough to walk. Once they were down safely, Duff and Lockey quickly followed in their footsteps and soon they were speeding down the road on the way to Boulder Community Hospital. They arrived at the emergency room and waited about an hour before a nurse took them back to an examination room. Cy had been right. Bowen needed six stitches, but he didn't appear to have a concussion, and the doctor assured them he would be fine after a little rest. He was stitched up, given a few pain pills, and sent on his way.

Bowen was quiet all the way back to the inn, not able to get that baby off of his mind, but his mind was working overtime. *I know what I saw. The baby disappeared right before my eyes. It couldn't have been....* Bowen shook his head, wincing at the pain. It seemed so real.

"Hey, Duff?" Bowen asked quietly.

"Yeah."

With no other clear explanation, Bowen finally asked the only question that had been preying on his mind. "When you see things like premonitions or entities or... spirits, do they look like real people or things?"

"Sometimes they do and sometimes they don't. It all depends. I guess I don't have to ask why."

"I know I saw this girl holding a baby. I thought it was a real person standing there, but when she threw the baby and it disappeared when I reached for it, I knew it couldn't have been real. I just can't shake the feeling this somehow has something to do with me."

He felt Cy's hand on his and suddenly he felt better. "It's all right. We'll figure it out."

Bowen looked at Duff through teary eyes. "My heart aches for that baby and it wasn't even real. Do you think you're rubbing off on me or projecting... or whatever it is you do, because I'm telling you, this feels—" He squeezed Cy's hand. "—very creepy."

Duff cleared his throat. "Who knows? I've been told everyone has a certain level of psychic abilities, some stronger than others, but you have to work at your abilities to make them stronger."

The Mystery of Ruby Lode

Bowen turned toward Duff and arched a brow. "If this is what you go through on a daily basis, I don't want any part of it."

Duff shook his head. "It's not for us to decide. It's a gift, and we can choose to use it or choose to ignore it, but sometimes the entity trying to communicate with you is so strong and wants to communicate so badly, you can't help but hear them."

"But why me? What does a woman throwing a baby away have to do with me? Why not try to communicate through you?"

"I can't answer that, Bo. I'm sorry."

"Maybe I'll feel better after some sleep."

Cy squeezed him again. "I'm sure you will, baby. Let's get you back to the inn and to bed. You'll feel much better in the morning."

By the time they left the hospital, it was three in the afternoon, and everyone but Bowen was starving. They ran by a drive-thru and picked up burgers and fries before heading back to the inn. While the guys ate in Lockey and Duff's room, Bowen decided to rest for a while. He lay on the bed, careful not to aggravate his stitches, and closed his eyes. He immediately saw the woman and the child. He opened them again, replaying everything in his head over and over. *Man, it was all so real.* He closed his eyes, and this time he willed himself to block everything out and just get some sleep. The pain pill must have kicked in because within minutes he began to fade into a deep sleep.

HE WAS startled out of his sleep by a whistle blowing. He was suddenly sitting on wooden bleachers, watching a football game. The referee had just taken the football away from one of the players, and they retreated into a huddle. Four girls in black-and-gold cheerleader uniforms with a big T on the chest raised their pompoms into the air and began to chant. "Pork chop, pork chop, greasy, greasy, we can beat your team easy, easy. Gooo, Trojans!" The whistle blew again, and two teams lined up for the next play. He heard the quarterback yell "hike" and the play was in motion. The opposite team was rushing the quarterback, and he saw an opening and took off for the goal line. He ran like a track star and crossed the goal line with no less than eight players chasing him. He threw the ball to the ground in a celebratory move as the cheerleaders threw their pompoms into the air and jumped up and down. The quarterback ran to the sidelines and picked up one of the cheerleaders, then kissed her on the lips while he spun her around in his arms. Shocked, Bo recognized her immediately as the girl at the mine. Soon the whistle blew, and the quarterback was again on the field.

The scene suddenly changed and he was in the front seat of a car watching the quarterback and the cheerleader making out in the backseat. The quarterback's hands were up her uniform and she was throwing her head back in ecstasy. She moaned and pushed into his hands as he fondled her breasts. He unbuttoned his blue jeans, forced the zipper down, and pulled out his fully erect dick. He lifted her skirt and positioned himself at her opening. "No," she whispered. "I-I can't." He pushed further into her. "No, stop," she yelled as she attempted to push him away. He pinned her arms back against the car seat and pushed all the way in. She cried and begged him to stop, but it was no use. He thrust into her over and over again. Bowen yelled "No! Stop!" but no sound came out. He tried to pull the guy off of her, but it was like he was somehow watching from a distance and he just couldn't reach her. Then the quarterback threw his head back and moaned as he shot his load and fell on top of the cheerleader. She pushed him off of her and started kicking with her feet. She caught him in the jaw and chest and sent the last blow right to his balls. He bent in half and wailed in pain as she finished him off with one last kick to the head. She struggled to find the door handle to free herself from the confines of the backseat, and when she finally did, she forced her shoulder into the door and it flew open. She crawled out of the car and fell to the dirt below. The quarterback regained his senses and hopped into the front seat just as she was crawling out of the back. He started the car and peeled off a layer of tire treads heading down the dark road. Bowen found himself standing in front of the weeping girl and not knowing what to do. She wiped the tears from her eyes in a defiant move and used her skirt to wipe the blood that was now running down her leg. "I will never let another man touch me," she mumbled over and over through her sobs.

Bowen blinked and that scene ended, and he was now in a hospital room and the pregnant cheerleader was lying in a hospital bed with her feet up in stirrups. The doctor was telling her to push and she was screaming to the doctor and nurse to get the fucking thing out of her. Finally, the baby popped out and she threw herself back on the hospital bed and closed her eyes. The nurse cut the cord, cleaned the baby, and tried to place him on her bosom, but she pushed the baby away.

"It's a boy," the nurse explained.

"That fucking thing ruined my life and I hate it. Take it away. I never want to see it again. Let him make someone else's life miserable." The nurse took the baby away, and it was then that Bowen saw the birthmark on the baby's cheek. His heart sank to his feet. The baby boy he was staring at was him. The cheerleader and the quarterback were his birth parents and neither of them wanted him.

HE WOKE up with tears running down his face and what felt like a huge gaping hole in his heart. *It was a dream, it was only a dream,* he tried to convince himself. *But why did the pain feel so real?* All his life, he'd known he'd been given up at birth, but he'd convinced himself there had to have been circumstances beyond his parents' control that forced them to give him away. But his dream seemed so real, and lying alone in a dark hotel room, he convinced himself to accept it as the truth. He closed his eyes and silently wept for the infant version of himself, feeling more alone than he'd ever felt in any foster home.

CY FINISHED his burger and fries, wadded up the wrappers, and placed them in the empty bag. "What in the hell do you think happened out there?" But before he allowed them to answer, he spoke again.

"You guys know Bowen. He would never do anything stupid like leaping off of a fucking mountain, for Pete's sake. He must have seen something."

"Maybe he did," Duff agreed.

"I believe him," Lockey added. "He wouldn't make this shit up."

Cy nodded. "I believe him too. But it's just so weird."

Duff stood up, seeming a little annoyed. "What's so weird about it? I go through this shit all the time."

Cy looked back and forth between Duff and Lockey. "It's not weird for you, but it sure is for Bowen."

"Good point," Lockey offered.

Duff started pacing around the room. "Hey, Lockey, you wanna ride back out there with me? I want to see if I can pick up on anything."

"Sure, I'll go."

"I'll stay here and keep an eye on Bowen," Cy offered. "I just don't want to leave him."

"No problem, we'll be back in a couple of hours."

After Lockey and Duff left to go back to the mine, Cy tiptoed into his and Bo's room, and eased into bed. In the dark, he gently kissed Bowen on the cheek and tasted the wet, slightly salty tears. His heart dropped into his stomach and dread filled his being. "Bo, what's wrong? Are you in pain?"

Bowen shook his head from side to side, but didn't respond.

Cy immediately put his arms around Bowen and drew him close. "It's okay, baby, tell me what's wrong."

Bowen pulled away from him, rolled over, and turned on the lamp on the bedside table. In the dimly lit room, Cy could see Bowen's swollen red eyes and knew he'd been crying for a while.

Bowen grabbed a tissue from the bedside table, wiped his eyes, and blew his nose before turning back to Cy and snuggling against him with his head on Cy's chest. "It was just a stupid dream."

"Do you want to tell me about it?"

"It's stupid really. I don't know why I'm letting it get to me. It was just a dream."

"Baby, dreams can seem awful real sometime. What was it about?"

"My birth parents."

Cy tensed just a little out of concern. He knew being given up at birth was a sensitive issue for Bowen. It was an issue he didn't discuss much but one they'd talked about a few times over the years. Not knowing the circumstances of how and why he was given up had made Bowen a very insecure kid, and going from one foster family to another didn't help his self-esteem. But Bowen had told Cy that on his eighteenth birthday, as part of his rite of passage to manhood, he'd put the entire thing behind him, and he wasn't going to allow the actions of his birth parents to control who he was and how he lived his life as an adult. He'd wasted too many years as a child being insecure, lonely, scared, and always afraid of rejection. And to Bowen's credit, he'd done just that. He was the most well-adjusted, loving, and secure person Cy had ever known. At least, Cy thought he was.

"What about your birth parents?"

Bowen described the entire dream from start to finish and Cy's heart broke with each crack of Bo's voice as he recounted the tale scene by scene.

Cy put his bent finger under Bo's chin, lifted his head until their eyes met. "Look at me, Bowen McAlister. It was just a dream, probably brought on by the blow to your head. You can't take a dream as the gospel truth."

"I know you're right, but it was so damn real. And that might be exactly how it happened."

"And it might not, Bo. Don't allow a crazy dream to take control of your emotions."

"You're right, I know you're right, but…." Bowen stopped midsentence.

"But nothing. Look, baby, we don't know the circumstances around your birth, but what we do know is that I'm right here, and you are more loved and wanted than you can ever know. That's not ever going to change. I love you."

Cy leaned in and gently kissed Bo's waiting lips. He watched Bowen close his eyes, heard his sigh of relief, and he knew he'd finally gotten through to him.

Cy felt him relax in his arms. "Thank you. With each passing day, I love you more and more. I hope you know that, Cy."

Cy smiled. "Of course I know that, but it sure is nice to hear."

He kissed Bowen again, and they slid down into a spooning position with Cy's arms wrapped tightly around Bowen's waist.

Chapter FIVE

LOCKEY and Duff came to a stop at the end of the dirt road leading to the mine. It was almost dusk, and the sun was projecting purple, orange, and red rays onto the massive fluffy clouds in the background of the mountain range. They got out of the Jeep, and Duff took a deep breath of clean mountain air as he climbed onto the hood, leaned back on the windshield, crossed his arms over his chest, and closed his eyes.

Duff could hear the continuous scuffling sound of boots against dirt. He cocked open one eye and saw Lockey pacing back and forth in front of the Jeep, hands in his pockets and a worried look on his face.

"Lockey, it's not easy to concentrate with all that pacing."

"Do you have anything yet?"

Duff laughed. "You know it doesn't work like that. Either take a walk or sit in the Jeep, but please give me a few minutes of silence."

Lockey looked a little offended but turned on his heel and headed in the opposite direction.

Duff closed his eyes and again tried to focus on the mine or anything he might pick up. Ten minutes passed with nothing, and he was about to give up when he saw the usual flash in his head he always glimpsed right before a vision. Duff never knew the form a vision might take, but this time when the flash was gone, he was back in the childhood bedroom he'd been forced to share with his older stepbrother. The teenager, who was very upset that he had to leave the privacy of his own bedroom and share with his new younger family member, was yelling at him for ruining everything, which was a daily occurrence. As Duff looked on in his mind, he tried to pull himself away from the vision to see if he could determine the source. He could sense another presence but couldn't identify it. It seemed to be coming from somewhere deep within the mine.

Minutes or hours later, he didn't know which, he was jarred back to his vision. Back in his bedroom, his stepbrother was unzipping his pants and pulling his dick out. He saw himself as a child being forced down to his knees and being held by the hair as he gagged and gasped for air every time his stepbrother pulled his erect dick out of his mouth and forced his way back in. As his stepbrother shot down his throat, he gagged and coughed, come running down his chin and neck. His small frame went limp when his stepbrother slapped him across the back of the head and released him. When he came to, his stepbrother told him if he ever said a word to anyone about their recurring little incidents, he would kill him.

Watching himself unconscious on the floor of his old bedroom with come all over his face, chin, and neck left him feeling ashamed and humiliated. On a daily basis, he remembered the abuse he'd suffered at the hands of his stepbrother, but he'd never seen it in a vision like this. His heart ached for the younger Duff, and he cursed himself for not doing something about it back then. He was slowly coming back to reality, and when he finally opened his eyes, Lockey was on top of him with both hands on his biceps, shaking him relentlessly.

"Thank God, Duff, I thought you were dead." Duff could see Lockey was visibly distraught, and his hands were shaking. But before he could respond, Lockey had him in a death grip and his lips were suddenly covering Duff's. At first the kiss was frantic and fearful, and then it became slower and more tender. Lockey's tongue pressed against Duff's lips, and without knowing why, he opened to him. They kissed passionately, and when the kiss ended, Duff stared up at Lockey and smiled. "If I thought having a vision in front of you would have gotten me kissed like that, I would have done it a long time ago."

Lockey, caught off guard and realizing what he'd just done, turned beet red, slowly released Duff, and climbed off the hood of the Jeep.

He again paced back and forth. "I-I'm sorry, Duff. I don't know what came over me."

"It's okay, Lockey. It's the most action I've had since my last nightmare."

Lockey smiled a little and his cockiness seemed to return. "That good, huh?"

"I said it was the most action I've had in a long time, not the best."

Lockey grabbed his chest. "Right to the heart, Duff, right to the heart."

"Yeah, well, old habits die hard."

"What in the hell just happened to you? Where did you go?"

"I'd been trying to pick up on some kind of energy or entity around the mine, and I was just about to give up when right out of nowhere, it hit me."

"What hit you?"

"Let's go and I'll explain everything in the car."

On the way back to the inn, Duff explained what he'd experienced in his vision and how he sensed the source of the vision was coming from somewhere in the mine.

"Dude, did your stepbrother actually do that shit to you?" Lockey whispered.

"That and a whole lot more," Duff confessed in an almost embarrassed tone. "The fact is, I've never told anyone about the crap I went through after my mother died."

"Come on, man, we've been friends for going on ten years. I think we should know this shit."

"The past is the past, and nothing I can say or do now is going to change it."

"Yeah, but Duff, that's an awful lot of baggage to carry around by yourself. Why didn't you ever tell us?"

Duff thought for a minute before he answered. He wanted to say no one had ever cared enough about him to ask, but he knew that wasn't true. Lockey, Cy, and Bowen—they all cared, but none of them had ever asked him about his childhood. They'd all shared stories of being a kid and growing up, but they'd never once noticed he'd never volunteered any information about his life after his mother died.

"Come on, Duff, say something."

Duff couldn't speak. Feelings of emotional and physical abandonment swirled throughout his being and the pain of not feeling loved by his father or his new family rushed back at him. He was on the verge of becoming very emotional, and he didn't want that to happen, especially in front of Lockey. He swallowed the lump in his throat and finally managed to choke out, "Because no one's ever asked." But he regretted saying it the minute the words left his mouth.

The Jeep was silent. Duff turned to Lockey and saw tears were building in his eyes. Lockey must have sensed Duff's gaze because he quickly looked away, staring out of the window into the darkness.

Duff reached out and put his hand on Lockey's knee. "That was a cheap shot. I'm sorry."

Lockey covered Duff's hand with his own. "It wasn't a cheap shot. It was spot-on, and I really don't know what to say except that I'm the sorry one. For the last ten years, I've been so caught up in my life and feeding my own ego, I never paid much attention to the people I care about."

The Mystery of Ruby Lode

"Come on, Lockey, you can't blame yourself for not knowing everything about me. I don't blame you. Besides, if I would have given you any hints, I know you would have been there for me."

"It must have really bothered you, knowing the way you feel about Cy, not to share that with him."

"What Cy and I had was very brief and may or may not have turned into something lasting, but once he met Bowen, any romantic thoughts he had about me were gone instantly. And don't get me wrong; I'm glad they are so happy. Those two were tailor-made for each other, and I wouldn't, no matter how painful, have it any other way."

Duff glanced out of the corner of his eye and Lockey was still staring out of the window. He squeezed Lockey's knee. "I thank God everyday we've remained friends. More than friends, you guys feel like the only real family I've ever had. I would never allow anything to come between us, not our past and certainly not my stupid feelings for Cy, and they are just that, stupid! I'm a grown man, for Pete's sake. Cy is happy with Bowen and it's time for me to be happy too."

Duff suddenly felt Lockey's damp eyes glaring at him. "Do you mean that?"

He kept his eyes on the road, one hand on the wheel and the other still on Lockey's knee, although he didn't know why he hadn't moved it.

"Yeah, why?"

"Pull over," Lockey said.

"What do you mean 'pull over'?"

"Just pull over."

Duff pulled onto the shoulder of the road and put the Jeep in park. Lockey turned to him and placed his hand on Duff's face and drew him close. "I'm sorry for not being a better friend." He leaned in and Duff felt Lockey's lips brush gently against his. Slow gentle kisses covered his lips, face, and neck.

Lockey pulled back and smiled. "When I kissed you on the hood of the Jeep back there, it was out of panic and fear, but this time it was because I wanted to." Lockey leaned back into his seat. "We can go now."

Duff was sure he must look like the proverbial deer in the headlights. He smiled and trembled for a second at the simplicity of what had just happened. He put the Jeep in drive and off they went as butterflies danced around Duff's stomach. He shook his head from side to side. *What in the hell is happening around here?*

They arrived back at the inn, and when they got to their room, Bowen was up. Both he and Cy were dressed for dinner.

"How's the head?" Duff asked when Bowen came into their room.

"Not bad, but those were some killer pain meds. I had some crazy-ass dreams."

Cy came up behind Bowen and slipped his arms around his waist. "How'd it go out there?" Cy asked.

"Very interesting," Duff admitted, looking at Lockey.

"I'll say," Lockey added, exchanging a smile.

"Okay, you two, what's going on? You both look like the cat that ate the canary."

"I think there's some negative energy or entity in that mine. I don't know who he or she is and I don't know what it wants, but they're playing some pretty serious mind games."

Cy released his arms from Bowen's waist and moved to stand next to him. "Like what?"

Duff explained to Cy and Bowen what he'd experienced at the mine. He left out the part about the passionate kiss on the hood, but told them everything else.

"My God, Duff! You were forced to blow your stepbrother?"

"Repeatedly. Among other things."

Bowen suddenly felt silly for feeling sorry for himself. "I'm really sorry, man," he offered. "That must have really been awful."

Duff looked down. "Yeah, it wasn't fun, but what's done is done." He desperately wanted to change the subject and not relive the details of his childhood again right here in front of his friends, so he said the first thing that came to his mind. "Hey, can we go and get something to eat so we can come up with a game plan?"

Realizing Duff was trying to avoid talking about his past, Cy reached over to pick up the phone. "Excellent idea. I'll call the concierge and see if they can suggest some place close by." They all waited while Cy spoke to the concierge.

"That's perfect. Thank you very much," Cy said then hung up the phone. "They suggested a place down the block called the Flagstaff House."

"Perfect, we can walk," Lockey said. "Let's go, I'm starved." Then he looked at Bowen and for the first time in a very long time, he remembered it was not all about him. "I'm sorry, Bowen. Do you feel up to walking?"

Cy looked at Bowen then Duff and finally settled his gaze on Lockey. "Who in the hell are you and what have you done with Lockey?"

Lockey snickered. "Very funny! I guess I deserved that." He looked at Bowen with a raised brow.

"Yeah, I'm good to walk. Let's go."

The Flagstaff House was pretty busy, and it took them about twenty minutes to get a table. They placed their drink orders and silently checked out the menu.

Bowen broke the silence. "So, what's going on at that mine?"

Just then the waiter came back to take their food order. After they ordered, all heads turned to Duff with questioning looks.

Duff sighed. "Well, what we know for sure is that Bowen and I have had some interesting things happening to us since we've arrived. But before I tell you what I think is going on, we all need to think back and be very honest with ourselves and each other about anything odd:

premonitions, dreams, feelings we might have had right before or during this trip."

Cy and Bowen looked at each other with confused expressions.

Duff waved his hand in the air. "I'll go first, and Lockey already knows this because he came in right in the middle of it."

Again Cy threw Bowen then Lockey a confused look.

"First of all," Duff said, "let me be perfectly clear that what I'm about to tell you was partly a dream and partly a psychic experience."

Cy and Bowen nodded.

Duff told Cy and Bowen the truth about the dream he'd had the night they arrived. He recalled every detail again, confessing it was Cy coming on to him and raping him, not Lockey.

"Jeez, Duff, me coming on to you? You said it was Lockey."

"Come on, Cy, who is not important. What is important is, I think it was more of a controlled projection of what the entity wanted me to see."

"What entity? Who are we dealing with?" Bowen quietly asked.

"I don't know yet, but I guarantee we'll find out before we leave Boulder." Duff continued. "Look, guys, I said we have to be honest and that starts with me." Duff sighed and looked at Lockey. Lockey took his hand under the table, and Duff had to admit he liked the feeling of someone caring. "Negative entities usually go after emotional weak spots and always hit under the belt, so to speak."

Cy stared blankly at Duff. "What are you trying to say, Duff, that I'm an emotional weak spot where you're concerned?"

Duff felt Lockey squeeze his hand and he held on for dear life. *OMG, here I go!*

"Before I answer that, Cy, you and Bowen need to know I love you guys and would never do anything to ever come between you."

Cy stiffened in his seat. "What is that supposed to mean?"

"It means that I… uh, that I've sort of been carrying a torch for you since we dated way back in college."

"What!" Cy yelled. Everyone in the restaurant turned to look in their direction. "What?" he repeated in a lower tone.

"I'm sorry, Cy, and I know it's stupid, but it's just something I couldn't shake."

"You mean I'm something you couldn't shake."

Duff looked at Bowen. "I would never come between you guys. I can see how much you love and respect each other, and that means the world to me."

Bowen looked at Cy and then back to Duff. "Duff, I've suspected you've had a crush on Cy for a very long time, and—"

"Wait!" Cy said, raising his hand to stop the conversation. "You suspected this and never mentioned it to me?"

"Why mention it? I trust you completely and I trust Duff. Whatever Duff was dealing with was for Duff to deal with and none of our business. You never led him on, and he never acted inappropriately, that I'm aware of. I don't blame him. Besides, baby, I sort of understand. I could never get over you if you dumped me."

"Oh, thanks a lot," Duff said. "Now I was dumped."

Cy, ignoring Duff's last comment, took a deep breath and let it out. "Yeah, but it sure would have been nice if one of you would have clued me in."

"I'm sitting right here, guys," Duff grumbled. "I'm dealing with this and working through it with Lockey's help—"

"Wait!" Cy yelled yet again. "Lockey knew too?"

"He just found out last night."

"Oh, thank God," Cy whispered. "At least I wasn't the only totally blind, deaf, and dumb idiot in this bunch."

"Hey," Lockey said. "I resent that. In all honesty, I've been too wrapped up in my own life to pay attention to what any of you guys were going through."

Duff clapped his hands. "Hey, back to me. Can I please finish? I probably would have never brought this up ever if I didn't have a feeling we're dealing with something pretty strong here, and we need to face it head on. This entity has locked onto me—"

"And me," Bowen interrupted.

Surprised, Duff turned to Bowen. "What do you mean?"

Bowen looked at Cy and fidgeted a little, but started his story. "You guys already know I was given up for adoption at birth and spent eighteen years in foster care going from one family to another. But what you don't know is that all my life, I guess because I never knew why my birth parents gave me up, I've always had this deep-seated fear of rejection. Not knowing the circumstances surrounding my birth and wondering why my parents never wanted me has affected me more than I ever realized. I thought I'd dealt with those emotions and put them away, but I'm thinking not. Especially after this last episode."

Bowen recounted his dream about the cheerleader he'd seen at the mine and how she'd been raped and he was the unwanted result.

"This is getting too weird," Lockey said. "This thing, whatever it is, is going after us one by one."

"Two down and two to go," Duff mumbled. "Guys, this thing will sense and play off of our weaknesses and fears. It's all part of the energy it draws from us. When we're weak, it gets stronger."

Bowen placed his elbows on the table and rested his chin in his open hands. "But why us?"

Duff looked at all of them one by one. "I don't know yet, but maybe if the entity is in that mine, it wants to keep us out."

"So what do we do?" Bowen asked.

"We face it head on. As I said, while Lockey and I were out there, I sensed the energy coming from deep within the mine. I say we go down there like we planned and see what we find, both physically and spiritually. I have no idea why this entity latched on to us, and if it wants to try and keep us out of there for some reason, it will try to divide and conquer, possibly try to pit us against one another by playing on our insecurities. Anything to keep us out."

The Mystery of Ruby Lode

"Tomorrow," Bowen said, raising his fisted hand into the air, "we kick some ghost ass."

The others raised their fisted hands into the air as well and knuckle bumped.

When their meal finally came, they ate in virtual silence. Each man seemed lost in his own thoughts, but not willing to share just yet. The walk back to the inn was about the same. Duff noticed Lockey stayed by his side all the way home in a protective sort of posture, and that made him smile. No one had ever tried or even cared enough about him to be his protector, and, if he was being honest with himself, he liked it. But he still had lots of questions about Lockey's recent behavior. They'd known each other for ten years, and he'd never shown any romantic interest before. Why now?

When they got back to the inn, Bowen and Cy excused themselves immediately, which left the two of them standing in the foyer and Duff feeling awkward around Lockey for the first time in ten years.

"I'm gonna turn in. I'm pretty beat," Duff admitted.

Lockey smiled shyly. "Me too."

When they got to their room, Duff watched as Lockey sat on the edge of the bed and appeared to be having some sort of internal debate with himself. Duff, always being the caretaker of the group, pushed his awkward feelings aside and sat on the bed next to Lockey.

"Okay, Lockhart Dawson, it's just you and me now. What gives?"

Lockey opened his mouth to speak. "I...," he started, and then he shut it again.

Duff patted his knee. "It's okay, man. You know you can tell me anything, right?"

Lockey hesitated again and then turned and looked Duff right in the eye. "Over the last ten years, I've...," and he stopped again.

"You've what, Lockey?"

Lockey's bottom lip was starting to quiver and he looked a little pale. "I've given you so many subtle hints that I was interested in you, and you never ever acknowledged any of them. There, I've said it. Now tell me you're not interested and how lame I've been, and we can get this thing over with and get back to normal."

"What? Interested in me?" Duff was shocked, excited, and surprised all at once. He tried to think back over the past years to see if he could ever remember feeling as though Lockey was interested in him, but nothing came to mind. He shook his head in amazement.

"Yes, you! I figured you just weren't into me and didn't want to hurt my feelings."

Duff rubbed his hands together nervously. "Why would you be interested in me?"

"The whys don't matter, Duff," he said in a defeated tone. "I'll tell you about all the reasons later, but the now matters a lot."

Duff stuttered. "But… but… you can have any guy you want."

"Who cares how many guys I can have? Certainly not me. What's important to me right now is whether you dismissed my advances because you weren't interested or because you were in love with Cy."

"Wait! Hold on, Lockey! What advances? I don't remember you ever asking me on a date or even insinuating you might have the slightest interest in me."

Lockey was starting to get some color back now and was becoming a little more animated. He jumped up and threw his arms in the air. "Oh, come on, Duff. Are you serious? Were you so blinded by Cy that you were oblivious to everything and everyone around you?"

Duff thought about the question. "Maybe I was."

"Okay, now we're getting somewhere," Lockey insisted. "So let's take Cy out of the picture completely. If I told you I've had the biggest crush on you for the last ten years and I would love to see where it might go, what would you say?"

Duff chuckled. "Well, the first thing that comes to mind is—why?"

"I'm trying to be serious, Duff."

"Okay, I'm sorry. But it's hard to believe someone like you would be interested in someone like me."

"You really have no idea how that shy and charming demeanor of yours makes me weak in the knees. Not to mention the fact that you're hot as hell."

Not being able to keep still any longer, Duff stood and paced back and forth in the small hotel room. Those butterflies were back, and his heart was racing. "I'm really trying to wrap my head around this, I swear, but you and me?"

"Why is that so tough to wrap your head around?"

Duff looked up and down Lockey's tall, lean frame then settled on his dark-brown eyes. "When was the last time you looked in the mirror?"

"Ah, shit, Duff. I'd hoped that after all these years, you saw me as more than just a pretty face."

"Of course you are. You're the one smart enough to figure out that because I've spent the last ten years of my life with my head stuck up my ass, privately pining away for Cy, I didn't give you or anyone else a second look. I mean, don't get me wrong. I haven't been a saint. I got what I needed when I needed it, but it was never anything more than a physical thing."

"Okay, I get it, so you got laid when you needed to. No one would ever hold that against you."

"But… things have got to change," Duff mumbled almost to himself, still pacing back and forth. "I can't do this thing with Cy any longer. It's going to be the death of me."

Lockey jumped in front of Duff. "Stop pacing! You're making me dizzy." He took both of Duff's hands in his and looked him in the eyes. "Why now? Why do things have to change now?"

Duff looked up and closed his eyes. He thought hard about the question before he spoke, but he didn't really have a definitive answer. "I don't know for sure. Something happened to me at that mine. I don't know what, but something. But besides that, there are a couple of possibilities. You know, all along it's been like a fantasy to me that one day Cy and I, well you know, would be together, but now that they both know the truth about how I feel, it makes it more real. And thinking about it in real terms, I know it will never happen. Or the last possibility is that maybe… just maybe… it's because I'm finally tired of feeling second best."

Lockey linked his fingers behind Duff's neck and again looked him in the eye. "You should never be made to feel second best."

Duff broke eye contact and looked down at the floor. "But I've felt that way since my mother died, so it's all I know. I know it sounds crazy, but second best always felt comfortable and familiar, like where I'm always supposed to be."

"Good God, Duff, you deserve so much better than second best. And if you'll let me, I'll prove it to you."

Lockey's hands slipped from the back of his neck, and he ran his finger under Duff's chin. He lifted Duff's head until their eyes met again, and then Lockey passionately kissed him. Duff tensed; every muscle in his body froze. *Lockey wants me?* Slowly he relaxed and let himself be drawn into the warmth of the kiss. Lockey deepened it until heated passion was flowing between them. Duff's heart was pounding and doing backflips all the while his brain was overloading. He felt like if he didn't pick one or the other, he was going to explode, so he did what any gay male would do: he went for the heart and fuck the brain.

When the kiss ended, leaving them both a little breathless, he wanted to beg Lockey to do it again. But instead, he opened his eyes, and Lockey was smiling at him. "So, you never answered my earlier question."

Still reeling from the kiss, Duff's voice was shaky. "What question?"

Lockey huffed. "You know what question."

"How do you expect me to think after a kiss like that?"

"Stop being an ass, Duff, you know what question."

"Okay, okay, I'm sorry. Ask me again."

Lockey sighed. "Okay, I'm going on record this time... if I told you I've had the biggest crush on you for the last ten years and I would love to see where it... we... could go, what would you say?"

Duff thought hard and started pacing again.

Lockey threw his hands in the air. "Oh, never mind. Forget I said anything."

Duff stopped pacing and turned around. "I would say 'hell yeah'!"

"Really? Say it again!"

"I said... hell yeah!"

Duff almost lost the ability to breathe as Lockey's arms wrapped around him and squeezed him within an inch of his life.

He felt Lockey's hands clench his shirt and his warm full lips were soon smothering him with kisses. He was pushed backward, stopping only when his legs hit the bed. Suddenly, his shirt was being torn open and he heard the faint sound of buttons hitting the far walls. The next thing he knew, he was shirtless and flat on his back in the middle of the bed. Lockey straddled his waist and secured Duff's hands over his head. Lockey's face was buried in his neck, and whatever Lockey was doing was sending chills up and down his spine. His hands were suddenly released, and he took the opportunity to run his fingers through Lockey's dark-brown hair. But he knew Lockey was far from finished with him. Duff heard a moan as Lockey dropped down and began kissing and biting his way across Duff's chest. Lockey stopped on his left nipple and lightly nibbled and teased until it was as hard as his growing erection.

Lockey moved farther down his body until he was straddling Duff's knees. He unbuckled Duff's belt and struggled with the metal buttons of his button-fly jeans. When his belt and jeans were open, Duff watched as Lockey buried his nose in his crotch and inhaled deeply, making his shaft swell. Lockey looked up with heavy lidded eyes. "I've always wondered what your scent was like, and it's sexy as hell."

He watched Lockey slide down farther until he felt Lockey's ass hit his feet. Lockey backed off the bed and knelt on the floor while he untied Duff's boots and removed them one at a time, massaging each foot as he went. Lockey removed Duff's socks and reached up and grabbed his jeans at the ankles. Duff instinctively raised his hips off the bed as Lockey pulled his jeans down and off. Duff watched as Lockey folded his arms across his chest, licking his lips as he looked appreciatively at the growing erection tenting Duff's boxer briefs. Lockey's lust-filled gaze sent a shiver down his spine.

Duff pushed himself up to the head of the bed and leaned against the headboard, his heart pounding in anticipation. Lockey unfolded his arms and started unbuttoning his own shirt. He moved slowly and deliberately, undoing each button in a teasing motion, his gaze never wavering from Duff's eyes. Duff was hard as a rock, and his shaft throbbed painfully in anticipation as the sexy man in front of him finally unbuttoned the last button and pulled the shirt from his jeans. He slowly let the shirt slide down his shoulders and allowed it to fall to the floor. Lockey reached down, pulled his white T-shirt out of his jeans, and lazily pulled it over his shoulders and head, exposing his massive well-defined chest. Duff licked his lips, eager for what was to come. Lockey then propped his foot up on the end of the bed and leisurely untied his boot, again never taking his eyes off of Duff.

He removed his boots and socks and Duff's eyes grew wide as Lockey intentionally rubbed his hand over his bulging crotch a few times and then slowly unbuckled his belt and unzipped his jeans. Lockey pushed his jeans down over his hips. They fell to the floor and he stepped out of them. Duff thought about shifting positions to relieve the pressure, and then he saw Lockey's briefs were just as tented as his own. But before he could move, Lockey was again on the bed, lying flat on his stomach with his head buried in Duff's crotch. He nibbled at Duff's erection through his cotton underwear with just the right amount of pressure to make his toes curl.

The Mystery of Ruby Lode

They'd been friends for at least ten years, and over the years they'd had many personal conversations about sex, so Duff knew Lockey liked to bottom and wasn't the least bit ashamed of it. And that was just fine because Duff didn't bottom, but he sure as hell liked the top position, so the way he saw it, this was a marriage made in heaven. With that in mind, he slid down and pulled Lockey up until their lips met again and kissed him passionately. In a Superman-like move, he flipped Lockey over onto his back and ground their erections together as he continued the assault on his mouth. It was his turn now to show Lockey what he was made of, and he was going to take his time doing it. He gripped Lockey's wrists and raised his arms over his head and held them there. He buried his face in Lockey's left armpit and inhaled deeply, savoring his musky scent combined with the slight smell of perspiration. The scent and sensation aroused him more than he could ever have imagined, and the simple action sent throbs down to his groin. He continued licking across Lockey's chest, lightly brushing his teeth over the sensitive skin around his nipples, and over to the other armpit. He was encouraged to continue as he drew a guttural moan from his lover's lips.

He licked from Lockey's pit to his neck, tantalizing the tender skin beneath his touch. Another moan and an "Oh God, Duff," drove him down to the hairless, chiseled chest lying in front of him. He bit lightly on a perfectly round, tan, and erect nipple, causing Lockey to break his hands free and cup the back of Duff's head, pressing it into his nipple and forcing him to bite harder. He gently but forcefully pulled at Lockey's nipple with his teeth and licked it multiple times, stopping only when he felt the pressure on the back of his neck subside. He changed positions and moved on to the other nipple to offer equal torture.

His dick was now fighting the constraints of his underwear, and it was his turn to stand at the foot of the bed and put on a show. But as he made his way to the end of the bed, he slipped his index fingers into the waistband of Lockey's briefs and slid them off in one quick fluid motion. Lockey smiled. "Nice move," he whispered with a wink. "I'll need to remember that one."

Duff cocked an eyebrow. "And who are you going to use it on?"

Lockey grinned playfully and took a minute like he was thinking. After a brief pause, he whispered, "No one but you, babe."

Duff nodded as he stood at the foot of the bed and worked his briefs down over his protruding erection until the black cotton underwear was in a puddle on the floor. He stared at the man he was about to ravish and was rewarded with dark-brown eyes full of need. For the first time in more years than he cared to admit, he didn't imagine it was Cy he was about to love but saw Lockey for exactly who he was. His heart was suddenly free, and the liberated feeling was intoxicating. He was overtaken with lust and growled as he jumped back onto the bed and wrapped his full lips around Lockey's waiting erection. His lips encircled the shaft and slid down in one amazing gulp until he was inhaling his lover's musky scent. Lockey was thick and long, and Duff relaxed his throat and took him in all the way. His heart was pounding as Lockey's hands gently caressed the back of his head, encouraging him to continue. He languidly moved up and down, applying a gentle suction, and based on the moans escaping Lockey's mouth, he was doing something right. Duff rose up onto his knees, placed a hand on either side of Lockey to brace his upper body and continued his slow and steady sensual attack.

"Oh, my God, Duff, if you keep that up, I'm gonna lose it."

He came up and allowed Lockey to slip from his mouth. He tenderly kissed his way back up Lockey's ripped, lean torso until they were again face-to-face. He smiled and watched a grin form on Lockey's lips as well.

"I can't believe I missed out on doing this for the last ten years," Duff whispered.

"We both missed out, which means we have a lot of making up to do."

The Mystery of Ruby Lode

He buried his face in Lockey's neck once again and, like a silly teenager, fought the strongest desire to mark what was now his. *What the hell!* He gave in to the desire and sucked and nibbled, drawing up a perfect purple hickey on Lockey's neck while he wiggled beneath him. He pulled back and admired his handiwork. "That's gonna be perfect in the morning."

"Thanks a lot," Lockey teased.

"I aim to please," Duff responded as he kissed his way back down the chest and torso beneath him and pushed Lockey's legs back to savor the view. His hefty balls hung low and full, and Duff didn't waste any time going in for the kill. He licked and nipped at the soft, smoothly shaved skin and relished the feeling of Lockey's balls rolling around his mouth when he took them in. He gently licked his way down to the opening just below and heard a gasp when he focused his attentions on the sensitive area. Lockey's musky scent filled his senses again as he ran his tongue around the opening, gently probing and teasing. He readjusted Lockey's legs and rested them on top of his shoulders, which freed his hands to torment him in other ways. When Lockey was well lubricated with saliva, he slowly breached the opening with his forefinger, and his lover's torso arched completely off of the bed. He took that as a sign he should continue, and he did. He gradually added a second finger, which drew another gasp out of Lockey, who was now gyrating and pushing onto his fingers. He searched for just the right spot and Lockey yelled, "There, oh, my God, right there." He massaged the small bump, which drew moans and a "hell yeah" out of his partner.

"Lockey, do you have lube and condoms?"

"In my shaving kit on the vanity in the bathroom."

"I thought they took that at the airport?"

"They did, but I bought more at the sundry shop at the air mattress's hotel last night."

"Thank God."

"And… Duff?"

"Yeah?"

"Hurry."

Duff smiled as he jumped off of the bed and ran for the bathroom. When he returned, Lockey was already stroking his dick and stretching himself with his own fingers. He stared at the sight in front of him and guessed that if he even looked at his dick now, he would come immediately. He fought the urge and focused long enough to slide the condom on and position himself at his lover's opening. He dispensed some lube into his hand and coated the condom along with Lockey's dick. Then he applied lube to the waiting hole and easily slid two fingers, then three, into Lockey to make sure he was ready.

He removed his fingers and pressed the head of his dick against Lockey's hole, easily pressing his way in.

"Give me a second," Lockey whispered as he fisted the sheets and breathed through the breach and initial burn. He followed Lockey's lead as he now guided Duff with his thighs. Suddenly, Lockey pulled Duff toward him, which pushed his ass against the intrusion, and took him in all the way. "Yeah," Lockey moaned, holding Duff tightly against him.

Lockey stroked his dick with one hand, putting the other hand behind his head, and smiling. "Ride me, cowboy."

Duff laughed. "I guarantee this won't be any eight-second ride."

"I'm counting on it."

Duff slowly started to move with short, even strokes at first, and Lockey didn't disappoint. He rose to every thrust and pushed into them with a purpose. Duff was on fire. The sight of his dick sliding in and out of Lockey's tight opening was almost more than he could take. He closed his eyes as he fucked Lockey into the headboard.

"Open your eyes, Duff. I want to make sure you see it's me you're fucking and not Cy."

Duff opened his eyes and leaned down and covered Lockey's lips with his own, partly to reassure him he knew damn well who he was with, but mostly just because he wanted to do it. "I'm well aware of who I'm fucking, and it's certainly not Cy. The only real issue I'm having right now is trying to keep from coming and wondering why in the hell it took me so long to see you standing right in front of me."

Lockey beamed. "Who cares how long it took? We have each other now."

Duff leaned up, grabbed Lockey by the ankles, and held his legs straight up in the air, deciding now was the time to bring it home. He pulled almost all the way out and easily slid back in to the hilt. Lockey moaned as he turned his head from side to side. Duff continued fucking Lockey with long steady strokes until he saw Lockey's muscles tense and felt his ass tighten around his dick. Lockey shot his first spurt, which landed on his chest, with his second and third shots covering his abdomen. Duff watched him squeeze the last drop of come from his spent dick and lay his head back down on the pillow.

Duff pumped harder, in then out, until he felt the orgasm building in his toes and working its way up his spine, setting each nerve tingling and on fire. Every one of his own muscles tensed, and he called Lockey's name as he shot his load into the condom deep inside Lockey's gut. Duff continued fucking him hard until he was certain there wasn't a drop left inside him. He dropped down on top of his lover and then attempted to catch his breath.

"Oh, my God, Lockey, that was incredible," he said, once he was able to speak.

Lockey threw his arms around his neck and they both moaned when Duff slid out of him. He planted a kiss on Lockey's lips and hopped out of the bed, removing the condom as he made his way to the bathroom. He came back with a warm, wet cloth and cleaned his lover's torso. When he climbed back in bed, Lockey burrowed into Duff's arms and rested his head on Duff's chest.

Duff wrapped his arms tightly around Lockey. "That was really hot. I can't believe what I've been missing. I feel like such a fool pining away for Cy for all these years when you were right here under my nose."

Lockey held on a little tighter. "That's in the past. We have the rest of our lives to see where this is going, and I'm gonna enjoy the hell out of the ride."

Duff ran his fingers through Lockey's brown locks. "Me too. But we better get some sleep or we're not going to be worth crap for our first day in the mine. Good night, Lock."

"'Night, Duff."

"And Lockey."

"Yeah?"

"Thanks."

"For what?"

"For making me see what was right in front of me."

"Oh, that. You're welcome, big guy."

Chapter SIX

THE next morning, Duff was awakened by gentle kisses on his back and shoulders. When he rolled over and opened his eyes, Lockey was dressed and sitting on the edge of the bed. "Wake up, sleepyhead."

Duff blinked his eyes and tried to focus on the alarm clock. "What time is it?"

Lockey glanced at his watch. "Six thirty."

"Holy shit, we're supposed to be ready by seven."

"That's why I got up and showered, so you could sleep a little longer."

Duff smiled but didn't say anything. *I could get used to this.*

He once again felt warm lips caressing his shoulder, then a quick bite. "Now up and at 'em, big guy."

He pulled the covers back and froze when he quickly remembered he wasn't wearing any clothes. He swallowed the lump in his throat, hopped up, and walked toward the bathroom, doing his best to ignore the catcalls from Lockey.

About a half hour later, still in the bathroom, Duff heard a series of knocks on the adjoining door and Bowen yelling for the ladies to get a move on.

Lockey opened the door. "What did I tell you about calling me a lady?"

Bowen stopped dead in his tracks. "Whoa! Either someone went out last night and got lucky or this inn has leeches, or, even worse, vampires. Dude, something's been sucking on your neck, big time."

Lockey smiled proudly and opened his shirt collar to give Bowen a better look. "Nice, huh?"

"Sure, for a teenage schoolgirl."

"Come on, Bo, give me a break. Just 'cause you're stuck sleeping with Cyrus every night doesn't mean you have to be mean to me."

"What? All I heard is 'stuck sleeping with Cyrus,' and I don't think I like where this is going," Cy joked as he walked into the room and stopped dead in his tracks at the sight of the purple mark on Lockey's neck. He took a moment to study the bruised skin. "What in the hell got a hold of you?"

Duff popped out of the bathroom with a towel around his waist and saw Cy and Bowen staring at Lockey's neck.

"Oh, Jesus." *We are so busted.* "What's up?" he asked nonchalantly as he walked over to his suitcase and grabbed some underwear, attempting to slip them on without removing his towel.

"We're just admiring Lockey's battle wounds."

Lockey smiled proudly, tilting his head to the side to give them a better view.

Bowen leaned on the doorframe, folded his arms across his chest, and crossed his feet at the ankles. "Soooo? Are you going to give us the usual gory details?"

Duff was trying to act like he wasn't listening, but he grunted and froze with his underwear at his ankles. He shot Lockey a pleading glance, hoping for the best, but preparing for the worst.

"Sorry, boys, but I don't kiss and tell."

The Mystery of Ruby Lode

Duff sighed with relief and pulled his underwear up.

"Since when?" Cy and Bowen said in unison.

Duff froze again and held his breath. *Lord, please help me.*

"Since Duff is really shy and doesn't want you to know it came from him."

Duff swallowed hard, pulled his underwear completely up and glared at Lockey with the fiercest look he could muster.

"What?" Cy and Bowen said, once again in unison.

Duff grumbled. "Okay, fine. It was me. You satisfied now?"

Cy folded his arms, put his hand on his chin, and walked around the room, studying, looking between Duff and Lockey. "My, my, Duff, you do have a certain glow about you this morning."

Lockey walked over and stood next to Duff. "All right, guys, you've had your fun. Give him a break. It was all my idea anyway."

Duff straightened. "It was not," he protested. "It was mutual."

Cy hopped on the bed and leaned against the headboard, a broad smile covering his face. "I knew it. I just knew there was something going on between you two."

Duff cocked his head to the side in confusion. "What do you mean 'going on'? It all just happened last night."

"Yeah, but I've had a feeling Lockey has a thing for you for quite some time."

Duff stomped his foot in frustration. "You knew? Why doesn't anyone ever tell me anything?"

"I guess for the same reason you didn't tell me you still had the hots for me. And speaking of, how much does this have to do with me and what you confessed last night?" Cy teased. "I know I must be very hard to get over, but it didn't take you very long—and with Mr. One-Night-Stand of all people?" he joked as he pointed to Lockey.

Bowen sat on the bed next to Cy. "Okay, you two, what do you have to say for yourselves?"

Duff again walked over to his suitcase. "Can I at least put some clothes on first?" He slid on his blue jeans, pulled a T-shirt over his head, and took a deep breath as Lockey took his hand and led him to the other bed. They sat down, hand-in-hand, facing Cy and Bowen, and filled them in.

When the story ended, Cy got up and started pacing. "Wow, this is one of the most informative trips we've ever taken, isn't it, Bo?"

"I'll say," Bowen said with a smile.

"And how many trips do you think we've taken together?"

"I don't know. I'd say at least a hundred."

"And we're just learning that Duff's had a woody for me and Lockey's had a woody for Duff and neither one of them thought it was necessary to tell anyone about any of this until now."

"Yeah," Bowen said. "But hey, why doesn't anybody have a woody for me? I thought we were all for one and one for all."

Cy reached over and kissed Bowen on the cheek. "Don't worry, baby. I'll always have a woody for you."

"Thanks, hon."

Duff stood up. "Come on, guys, we are friends, the best of friends. A few little details were left out, is all. But that's behind us now. No more secrets."

"Unless you two have something to share," Lockey said, looking at Cy and Bowen.

"Oh, no, don't turn this on us," Cy teased.

"Look," Lockey reasoned. "If it weren't for that mine and the strange things that happened out there, none of this would have come out. And I for one am very happy it did." He looked at Duff. "And… just to show you there will be no more secrets, I want to make this promise to Duff in front of the two of you." Lockey took Duff's hand again. "If you'll give me the opportunity, I will try to make you the happiest man on earth and never allow you to feel like you are anything but number one."

The Mystery of Ruby Lode

Duff was speechless. He felt tears building up behind his eyes. No one since his mother had ever made him feel like he was important or anywhere near number one. He was pulled into a bear hug that nearly knocked the wind out of him, and he savored the moment.

"Well," Cy said to Bowen. "It looks like congratulations are in order." They both stood and made their way to Duff and Lockey and threw their arms around them.

"Good luck, you guys," Bowen said. "I know I speak for Cy as well when I tell you we wish you all the best."

"Thanks, guys," Duff said. "Now, can we get a little mine exploring done today?"

"I still don't know why no one but Cy has a woody for me," Bowen whined. "What's wrong with me? Am I ugly? I'm a nice guy, aren't I, Cy?" Bowen babbled as they walked into their room to get their backpacks.

ON THE way to the mine, the guys went over their plan, which was to explore the first shaft as it was the oldest of the three and see what they could find before they moved on to number two. Once again parked at the road below the mine, the guys unloaded the Jeep and started unpacking their gear.

Because mines are made up of vertical shafts and horizontal drifts, traversing from one to the other could be quite hazardous, and older mine workings might even contain pockets of what's called "blackdamp," which is an area of still air with low oxygen levels and high concentrations of methane, carbon monoxide, carbon dioxide, or hydrogen sulfide. As a safety precaution, they unpacked everything they imagined they would need and everyone starting suiting up. Bowen called out item after item, waiting for a confirmation from each one that their equipment was there and in good working condition.

"Helmet?"

Three checks.

"Headlamps?"

Three checks.

"Multi-gas detector?"

Three checks.

"Rappelling gear?"

Three checks.

"Flashlight?"

Three checks.

"Spare batteries?"

Three checks.

"Spare air tanks?"

"Check. Check. And check."

Satisfied that everyone was ready, Bowen held his fisted hand out. "All right, boys. Let's go spelunking."

Loaded down with their gear, the guys bumped knuckles and started the hour-and-a-half trek up to the mine's opening. As they climbed, Bowen kept glancing at the mountain where he'd seen the cheerleader, but there was no sign of any activity. Trying to get his head back in the game, he concentrated on the task at hand.

Knowing many of the mines out west were in such dry climates that the capping and shoring stayed fairly well preserved, he closely inspected Ruby Lode's entrance and surmised that the capping was dried out, almost petrified, but fairly secure. Once inside, he could determine how well the internal shoring had fared. In any case, for extra safety, he decided to secure the rappelling lines to the large boulder at the mine's opening instead of the capping.

Bowen used his cell phone to call the local authorities and let them know they were going down into the mine at exactly nine hundred hours and would explore the shaft marked Number One on the survey. When it was time to descend, he took the lead, followed by Lockey, with Duff and Cy pulling up the rear. The shaft was dug at about a thirty-degree angle, so they would need to rely heavily on their

The Mystery of Ruby Lode

rappelling gear for stability. Bowen flipped on his headlamp, backed into the mine's opening, positioned himself, legs apart, line wrapped around his waist, and began lowering himself down. The opening was fairly tight, but Bowen, being the smallest of the four, dropped down onto his stomach and had little to no trouble getting through the tight spot. As he got to his feet again, the shaft widened, and he reported his findings back up to the guys. Lockey was next and did exactly as Bowen. He backed down to the opening, positioned himself, and then started his descent. As he approached the tightest part of the mine, he dropped to his stomach and eased by mostly unscathed. "Wow, this is a tight fit," he yelled up to Duff. "You'll need to drop down onto your stomach and shimmy down, but it opens right up once you're through the opening."

"Got it," Duff replied and passed the info along to Cy.

Cy, on the other hand, was the tallest and bulkiest of the bunch. He did as the others and positioned himself at the opening, rappelled down a bit then dropped onto his stomach. He shimmied, but instead of sliding through as the others did, something on his gear belt caught and lodged him in the tight opening.

Not being able to move, his heart sank to his feet and horror spread throughout his veins. *I'm trapped!* He started kicking and flailing, trying to break free, but it was no use. It was almost like he was being held in place by the walls of the mine. Trying to fight the panic that was quickly taking over, he attempted to slow his heartbeat and breathe deeply and slowly. As dread filled every fiber of his being, he tried to gain his composure. *Calm down, Cyrus! You're not alone, everyone's right here.* He closed his eyes.

He was a small child, frightened and alone, whimpering in the dark. He hated being in the dark. Momma always left the nightlight on for him, but she must have forgotten to turn it on. He tried to get up to turn on the light, but no matter how hard he tried, he couldn't move his hands or feet. He tried to call his momma and daddy, but there was something in his mouth keeping the words from coming out. The room was moving and he rolled from side to side. It would stop quickly and then start moving again, making his stomach really hurt. He smelled something that reminded him of the time his momma had taken him with her to that place where they work on cars. He tried to listen for her or his daddy, but all he heard was the sound the car made when his momma drove him to kindergarten. Suddenly the room stopped moving again. He heard two loud slams and the roof opened. The light was bright and he squinted against it. He felt something on his face, and he couldn't breathe. His throat hurt and he wanted his momma. Everything faded to black.

    He woke in another dark room, but this time it wasn't moving. He didn't smell the car place, but he still couldn't move his arms and legs, and they were starting to hurt. When he realized he wasn't having a nightmare and he hadn't woken up safe and sound in his bed, he began to cry. When he had no more sobs left, he noticed a light in the dark space coming from a long crack along the floor. He heard low voices coming from the other side of the door and thought, *Mommy and Daddy! They've come for me*! He laid his head against the floor, doing his best to look through the crack. He blinked through the tears and looked for his momma. All he saw were two pairs of shiny black shoes moving back and forth, and he began to cry again. But something about the way the shoelaces bounced back and forth when the shoes moved caught his attention and he stopped long enough to hear his name. "Momma, Daddy, I'm here. Please turn on the light. Please come and get me." He screamed through the thing in his mouth when he felt something tugging on his feet. He kicked and fought to break free, but he couldn't really move. He heard his name again.

    "Cy! Cy! Relax, you're okay. It's Duff. I'm here. Just stop kicking and slide down." Duff tugged on his feet and he simply slid down into the larger section of the mineshaft.

    "I… I was stuck," Cy said through gasps. He tried to calm down and catch his breath, but he was on the verge of hyperventilating. "My gear belt got hooked on something and I was stuck."

The Mystery of Ruby Lode

"Cy, your gear belt was already through the tightest part, nothing was blocking your way," Duff tried to explain.

"I was stuck, goddammit," Cy yelled.

"Okay, okay," Duff said in a calming voice. "Let's just keep moving until we get to the bottom."

Bowen shined his flashlight up the shaft, and Cy was able to get back to his feet and rappel down to join them. When he got to the base of the shaft, Bowen caught him.

"What happened up there, baby?"

He wrapped his arms around Bowen and held on tightly. "I don't know. One minute I was sliding down like the rest of you and the next I was wedged in the small part of the shaft," Cy explained. "It was the strangest damned thing. I just panicked."

He was shivering from fear and held on to Bowen as if his life depended on it.

"You're okay. I've got you."

"No, no. It's not being stuck that has me so rattled." He removed his flashlight from his gear belt and flashed it around. He saw everyone's confused looks. "Well, maybe partly, but there's something else."

Now he really had their attention.

"How long was I stuck?"

"A minute tops," Duff answered. "Why?"

"While trying to calm down up there, I closed my eyes and had some sort of flashback that seemed to go on for at least twenty or thirty minutes."

Bowen's concern was now very evident on his face. "What do you mean by flashback?"

Duff touched Bowen's arm. "He's okay, Bo, just give him a second."

Bowen took a deep breath and nodded.

"Do you feel comfortable telling us about it?" Duff asked.

Cy hesitated briefly, but then started to slowly recount his experience, detail for detail. As he relived the story, his heart started racing, his palms were sweating, and he became nervous and uneasy.

D<small>UFF</small> paced back and forth, head down and arms folded, trying to analyze what had happened to Cyrus and what it all meant. *I haven't felt any presence in the mine. Could the entity be blocking my senses somehow? It must be pretty strong, and it's taking us on one by one. First my dream about Cy, then Bowen's experience with the cheerleader and my experience on the hood of the Jeep with my stepbrother, now Cy.* He stopped and turned when he heard Lockey's voice.

"Okay, the beginning sounds like you were maybe locked in the trunk of a car."

Bowen released Cy's hand and held it up to cover his nose. "And then that thing covering your face, it must have had chloroform or something similar to knock you out."

"And then the second part," Duff added. "It sounds like you were in a closet. Could you have been looking under a door?"

Bowen raised a finger in the air. "And the shoes, Cy, the shoes are significant. It's no secret you hate shoes with laces and never wear them, but you never understood why."

Lockey was listening and contributing, but he was also checking out their surroundings. He shined his flashlight in Cy's face. "What's this about you hating shoes with laces? Why didn't I know that?"

All three men flashed their lights in Lockey's face. "Do we really have to answer that?" Bowen said sarcastically.

Lockey rolled his eyes. "I guess not."

Cy thought back. "Yeah, but I always thought it was because I hate being restrained or confined to small spaces. I just thought everyone had their phobias and that was mine. I never thought about what may have caused it."

"And therein lies the next significant thing. In your flashback, you are bound and gagged, hence the fear of restraints. Cy, the next part of this is crucial. Could this be a flashback to something that actually happened to you when you were a kid?"

Cy thought before he answered. "I don't know the answer to that."

"Cy," Bowen said. "Think back. You said you didn't remember ever living on Long Island, but you moved from there when you were five years old. You should have had some memory of that time."

"I've tried and tried to remember something, anything, from that time, but there's just nothing in my memory," Cy explained.

"Do you think it's possible you're repressing something awful, like—and I hate to even say this out loud—but like a kidnapping or an abduction of some sort? Cy, could you have been kidnapped as a young child?"

Cy's knees nearly gave out. He caught himself and remained steady on his feet, but his hands were shaking terribly and he broke out in a cold sweat. "I don't know. How could my family have kept something like that from me? I just don't know." He racked his brain to try and remember any detail that might shed some light on the situation, but nothing came to the forefront. "Could I have blocked out something that significant for all these years? That… would explain my loss of memory before our family moved to Mississippi."

Cy did the best he could to remain composed and not let them see how much he was struggling with his emotions.

"Well," he teased. "You said the entity would go for our weak spots, and… if that really happened to me, that would certainly qualify as a weak spot. Don't you think?"

Bowen nervously hovered over Cy. "Baby, why don't you sit for a minute, or even better, why don't we just call it a day and come back tomorrow? I'll call the authorities and tell them we've finished for the day. What do you say, guys?"

Cy looked around and everyone was staring at him. "Absolutely not! We have a mine to explore, and I'm not going to think about anything except the task at hand right now." He inspected his surroundings by waving his flashlight around the chamber. It appeared to be about a six-foot-by-six-foot chamber with three main shafts, as was documented, heading off in different directions.

According to the little information they had on Ruby Lode, the shaft to the left was the first shaft dug. As was the norm during the period when this mine was dug, the miner would dig a vertical shaft heading down at about a thirty-degree angle and then horizontal drifts off of the main shaft until they struck whatever they were mining for. In this case, it was gold. If nothing was found in a particular drift, they would repeat the process until the entire area was mined with no results. If no signs of any precious metals were ever found, the mine would eventually be abandoned. In many cases, miners spent their entire life in their mines, always thinking the mother lode was just beyond the next drift. Most never found their big payload and died trying.

"Let's get this show on the road," Cy yelled as he nudged Bowen to go.

Duff noticed that when Cy spoke, he saw his breath as it left his mouth. The temperature rapidly changed, and a blast of frigid air filled the chamber, hovered, and then passed through as quick as it came.

"What in the hell? Did you guys feel that?" Bowen asked through chattering teeth.

Cy wrapped his arms around himself. "Hell, yeah, I felt that."

"Me too," Duff and Lockey said simultaneously.

Cy looked around again. "There's got to be an opening in one of these shafts to produce that kind of draft."

The Mystery of Ruby Lode

"We've experienced a hell of a lot of drafts over the years," Bowen added. "But that was the coldest blast of air I've ever felt in any mine I've ever been in."

"I agree," Cy added.

"Either way," Bowen suggested, "let's shake it off. I'm anxious to see what lies ahead."

They started down the first shaft with Bowen in the lead and Cy right behind him. Duff motioned for Lockey to go next as he wanted a few seconds quiet time to get a spiritual feel for the mine and everything in it. He felt a quick chill run down his spine but brushed it off as he watched the guys fall in line ahead of him. Lockey took one step before he stopped and turned around to wait for Duff. Bowen and Cy kept going, and Lockey yelled, "That's okay, guys, don't worry about us. We'll be fine back here. Just look back occasionally to make sure we're still alive."

"Oh, please, you sissies," Cy yelled. "You want to go first?"

"No way," Bowen insisted. "I've got the lead, and I want you up here with me so I can keep an eye on you."

Lockey waved them on. "Just go! I'm joking around, guys. We'll be fine."

Already planning on pulling up the rear, Duff watched as Bowen and Cy rounded the corner and the shaft changed direction. Duff motioned for Lockey to go ahead of him, but Lockey refused. "You go and I'll take the last position."

Lockey waited for Duff to join him, but Duff wouldn't budge. "No, you go. I want to hang back here for few minutes to see if I can sense any presence."

Lockey stood with his feet firmly in place and crossed his arms over his chest. "Then I'm staying right here with you."

He started to protest, but Lockey interrupted him. "Listen, Mr. Exorcist, no way am I allowing you to go all Linda Blair on me when you're back here alone."

Duff's heart was suddenly full, and he felt warm all over. *He wants to protect me.* "Okay, Lockey, but this newfound boyfriend thing is going to take a little getting used to."

Lockey looked a little hurt. "What do you mean by that?"

He took Lockey's hand. "It's not a bad thing. I've just been a loner all of my life, and I'm pretty used to it. I guess that's what happens when you're in love with someone who's not in love with you. You get used to taking care of yourself and learn not to rely on anyone who's not going to be there."

"But I'm here now, and I want to be there for you. And more importantly, I want you to count on me being there. I swear to you I'm gonna prove to you guys I'm not the self-absorbed asshole you think I am."

"You don't need to…."

"Prove anything?" Lockey interrupted. "The hell I don't. You guys think I'm a superficial, bed-hopping gym bunny who only cares about himself. I've had that reputation so long I just give you what you want and that way everyone is happy. You have someone to make fun of and I get a free pass to be an ass and a child when I'm with you. But you couldn't be further from the truth. Do I always pay attention to little things like the fact that Cy doesn't wear lace-up shoes? Hell no, but I get the important stuff." Lockey looked down to the floor and kicked the dirt with the toe of his boot. "I've never missed one of your birthdays. I'm always the first one there when one of you is sick and, to be perfectly honest, I'd take a bullet for any of you."

Duff released Lockey's hand and threw his arms around his neck. "I'm sorry," he whispered. "You're right on the money. We don't give you enough credit."

"Nothing to be sorry for," Lockey said as he wrapped his arms around Duff's waist. "You expected me to behave a certain way, so that's what I did. It worked for everyone."

"You ladies coming?" Bowen yelled from within the shaft.

The Mystery of Ruby Lode

"In a second," Duff yelled back as he pushed Lockey away and looked him directly in the eyes. "We're going to hang back for a few minutes to see if I can pick up anything. But, guys, stay in the main shaft until we join you."

"Will do," Bowen responded.

Duff lowered his head and closed his eyes. He felt Lockey squeeze his hand as he concentrated on letting his senses take the lead.

After a few minutes, he opened his eyes and looked at Lockey. "I'm getting something faint, like we're not alone, but nothing I can identify. Let's get farther into the shaft and see if it gets stronger."

Lockey kissed him on the cheek and took the lead as they walked hand in hand into the shaft to join Bowen and Cy.

With their headlamps and flashlights, the mine was well lit. It was damp and moist, but it wasn't the worst they'd ever been in by a long shot. Most of the shaft had about a six-foot clearance, and the shoring seemed to be very well preserved. But where the shaft intersected the drifts, the clearance dropped to about five feet or so to allow for extra shoring.

Their agreed-upon plan was to follow the first shaft to the end, and then work their way back and explore all the drifts until they were back at the main chamber.

They passed the first drift on their right, which looked like it led in the direction of the second shaft, and Lockey stopped dead in his tracks. "Did you see that?" he whispered.

"See what?"

"Just as we reached the opening and I shined my headlamp into the drift, I thought I saw something like a black shadow moving in the opposite direction."

"I didn't see anything. Bowen! Cy!" Duff yelled. "Where are you?"

"We're up here," Cy yelled back.

"Are you guys still in the main shaft?"

"Yeah, why?"

"Have you seen anything strange?"

"No, nothing out of the ordinary."

Duff felt a chill pass over him. "Let's keep going. I'm getting something a little stronger."

They moved deeper into the shaft, Lockey never releasing his hand. Duff could see the glow of Bowen and Cy's lights in the distance as they approached the next drift. It was on the left, and Lockey stopped when they reached the opening. Duff bent his knees to clear the shoring and looked directly into the drift as he shined his flashlight and headlamp deep down into the damp tunnel.

Lockey waited. "See anything?"

"Nothing," Duff replied as he straightened up.

"What about spiritually? Getting anything?"

"Not a thing. The feeling I picked up on earlier is gone. But let's keep going and see if I can pick it up again."

When they were about to intersect with the next drift, which was on the right, Duff stopped dead in his tracks and whispered, "Slow down, I'm starting to get something pretty strong."

Lockey inched toward the next drift with Duff right behind him. When they stepped in front of the opening, they both froze. "Jesus," Duff choked out.

From deep inside the drift, he saw a heavy black fog heading in their direction. As it surrounded them, he squeezed Lockey's freezing hand and was suddenly cold and clammy and very uncomfortable. Then as quickly as it came, it disappeared. Lockey's hand began to tremble in his.

"Lockey, you okay?"

"Yeah, I'm okay, but tell me you saw that?"

"Yeah, I saw it. But the fact that you saw it scares the hell out of me."

Lockey squeezed his hand again. "What in the hell was that?"

"Probably some sort of entity trying to manifest itself to get our attention."

The Mystery of Ruby Lode

"Well, it worked," Lockey added.

"Let's keep going, Lock. The sooner we're all together, the better."

Lockey started walking again. The next drift was on the left and they passed it by with no strange occurrences, no fog, nothing.

As they approached the third drift, which happened to be on the right again, Lockey stopped short of the opening. Duff ran into the back of him, and when he stepped back, the black fog was surrounding Lockey. Duff's stomach dropped to his feet, and he felt the blood drain out of his face. *Oh my God, Lockey!* The fog was swirling around Lockey and his eyes were staring straight ahead—no blinking, no movement, just a blank stare. "Lockey!"

Lockey didn't answer. Duff squeezed his hand again. "Lockey?"

Still nothing. His heart sank and fear crept into every fiber of his being. He was about to panic. "No!" he screamed. "Fight it, Lockey, fight it! Now, damn it!"

LOCKEY was seven years old, and his father stood in the doorway of his home yelling "Fight, Lockey, fight," as four boys were on top of him, kicking and punching him and calling him a fatass faggot. He remembered his father just yelling, not helping him, but yelling "Fight, Lockey, fight," over and over again. Instead of fighting, he curled up into the fetal position, closed his eyes, covered his face with his hands, and let the other boys beat the hell out of him.

DUFF placed both hands on Lockey's shoulders and shook the hell out of him. *I am not losing him.* He shook him again, *"Fight it, Lockey. Please, please fight it."* Still no response. Duff did the only thing he knew how to do. "Leave him alone!" he yelled. "I'm the one you want! Take me, you cowardly bastard, take me!"

YOUNG Lockey peeked through the fingers covering his face, and Duff was there pulling one of the boys off of him. Someone's helping me. Duff is helping me. Lockey slowly started to fight. He started kicking randomly and just happened to get one of the boys in the balls. With two off of him, he got to his feet and started swinging. "No!" he yelled. "Leave us alone!"

DUFF still had a death grip on Lockey's hand when it suddenly began to tremble. He felt the exact second the entity left Lockey's body and entered his. Having more experience dealing with the paranormal, he was able to keep it at bay until it gave up and withdrew. He heard Lockey gasp for air, and he started shaking uncontrollably. Cy and Bowen must have heard all the yelling because they came back to see what was going on.

Lockey dropped down to his knees and lowered his head.

"What's going on?" Bowen asked.

"He's had some paranormal experience. Just let me deal with him." Duff dropped down to Lockey's level. "Look at me. Lockey, look at me."

Lockey's eyes seemed to be coming back to life, and he appeared to be trying to focus on Duff.

Duff looked up at Cy and Bowen, standing there white as ghosts. *I need to bring him back now! I've got to get him talking about something, anything.* "It's okay, Lock, I'm here. Talk to me, Lockey. Tell me what happened." He kept snapping his fingers in front of Lockey's face until he finally locked in on him.

He blinked a few times and opened his mouth to say something, but closed it again like the words weren't quite ready to come out. He closed his eyes and then opened them again.

"Lockey, baby, tell me what happened," Duff pleaded.

He didn't respond immediately, but when he did, his voice was hoarse and squeaky. Never breaking eye contact with Duff, he said, "Thank you. You saved me. I can't believe you saved me." Duff assumed he was talking about drawing the spirit out of him.

"Are you okay?" Lockey asked.

Duff smiled. "Yeah, I'm fine. But please tell me what happened. I need to know everything."

Lockey, still totally focused on Duff, started talking. "I felt this freezing cold air swirling around my head, almost suffocating me, and then I felt the air enter my body through my chest and move through me. It took over my arms and legs, one by one. It seemed so foreign at first, and then it quickly consumed my senses. It was angry, but I felt a sadness at the same time, if that's possible. But there was something else; it took me back to when I was a kid and some bullies were beating me up and calling me a fat faggot. My dad stood and watched the entire thing and didn't help me. He just kept yelling 'Fight, Lockey, fight.' But Duff, you came and saved me. I heard my father yelling, over and over, 'Fight, Lockey, fight,' but then from the far off distance his voice turned into your voice and I heard you yelling at me to fight and in my flashback, you came and saved me."

IT SUDDENLY occurred to Duff that Lockey was thanking him for something he didn't really do. "I would have saved you, baby, if I knew that was happening to you."

Lockey had tears running down his face. "You gave me the courage to fight and I'll never forget that."

He squeezed Duff's hand. "But it felt like the two things were connected somehow. Whatever entered me was alone and scared as well, running from something. Not scared of us, but of something else, like it was guarding a deep dark secret, which it never wanted revealed. It was the strangest damn thing I've ever experienced. One second, we were two beings in one body, and the next he was gone. Duff, am I crazy? Did you feel it?"

Duff nodded. "Yeah, I drew it out of you and it entered me, but I was able to hold it at bay and it eventually gave up and withdrew. It's not that strong. It seems like a young spirit and not very experienced."

"I swear I felt some kind of connection with it. Do you think it will come back?"

Duff stood, helping Lockey to his feet. "From what I've been told, it takes a hell of a lot of energy for an entity to enter another. My guess is it will need time to recharge."

"You guys want to call it a day?" Bowen asked.

"No," Lockey said. "I want to go on. How far are we from the end of the shaft?"

Cy pointed down the passage. "About twenty yards."

"How many more drifts?" Duff asked.

"Two on the left and one on the right. Why?"

Duff was pacing again. "We encountered the entity only in the drifts on the right side of the shaft. And the drifts on the right side of the shaft all head in the direction of the second shaft. All my senses are telling me the energy source is coming from the area of the second shaft."

"I say we keep going," Lockey suggested. "If we get this shaft explored and documented today, we can go into the second shaft tomorrow."

"Are you sure?" Duff asked. "Do you feel up to it?"

Lockey looked at Cy. "How about you, Cy? I'm not the only one who's had an interesting day."

"I'm good. I say we do it."

Duff looked at Bowen and they both shrugged.

"Okay, let's go."

The Mystery of Ruby Lode

AGAIN Bowen took the lead and Duff pulled up the rear with Cy and Lockey safely between them. They made their way to the next drift on the left and stopped and waited. As Duff expected, nothing strange happened, so they kept going. Duff kept the guys moving at a steady pace until they approached the next drift, which was on the right.

"Take it slowly, Bo," Duff whispered.

Bowen did as he was told, cautiously stepping in front of the opening and stopping. Cy stepped right up to him as Lockey and Duff inched closer in.

Duff waited for something to happen, but there was no fog, no energy, nothing out of the ordinary.

Lockey reached back and touched Duff's arm. "Looks like you were right."

Duff sighed with relief and was just about to suggest they move on when they heard this rough moaning sound coming from deep within the drift.

The hair stood up on the back of his neck and goose bumps appeared all over his body. "Someone tell me they heard that."

"I heard it," Lockey confessed.

"Me too," Bowen added.

"And me," Cy acknowledged.

Lockey, as if being summoned, started walking into the drift.

"Wait!" Duff shouted.

Lockey froze. "I've got to go in there."

Duff pulled Lockey back. "Wait."

"Duff," Lockey whispered. "Don't you try and help spirits cross over?"

"Yeah, but...."

"Duff, there's something sad and lonely about this spirit, and I want to try and help."

"But, Lock, some spirits can harm you. They're not all good. You can't just rush in there and save it."

"It was inside of me, and I felt such pain and loneliness. I'd love for you to help me, but I'm going in either way."

"Ah, shit," Duff mumbled as he looked at Cy and Bowen with a pleading look.

They both shrugged, and he knew he was doomed.

Duff sighed again. "Okay, I'll do this for you, but... on my terms."

Lockey smiled. "Just tell me what to do."

"You will do nothing," Duff protested. "I'll take the lead, and I will try to communicate with it."

Lockey started to argue but Duff held up his hand.

"You have little to no chance of accomplishing anything without me, but you have to promise to listen to everything I say and do whatever I tell you."

Lockey was obviously thinking about his response when they heard another moan, louder this time.

Looking a little intimidated, Lockey sighed. "Okay, Duff, you win."

"Come on, Lock, it's not about winning or losing. It's about keeping everyone safe and trying to get this spirit to cross over."

Lockey took his hand and smiled. "I get it. Tell us what to do."

"Just stay behind me and if, for some reason, this entity enters my body and I can't keep it at bay," he looked at Cy and Bowen, "you do to me what I did to Lockey. Yell, scream, shake me, hit me if you have to, but bring me back."

Cy and Bowen nodded at him hesitantly.

"Okay, let's go."

Duff took the lead as he stepped into the drift. The headroom was not over five feet and they all had to duck to not hit their heads. Slowly, Duff traversed the drift as it wound its way deep into the mountain.

The Mystery of Ruby Lode

Suddenly all their lights went out, the drift became pitch black, and everyone froze. Duff felt a frigid blast of air blow past him as he pounded his flashlight into his open hand. "Did you feel that?"

"Oh, yeah," they responded in unison.

Duff heard them pounding their flashlights as well, and then all at once, all the lights came back on, including their headgear.

"It's playing with us," Duff explained. "Trying to make us nervous and catch us off guard."

Cy shined his light in Duff's face. "Well, it's working."

Duff chuckled. "Just stay as calm as you can."

He started moving forward and stopped again when he heard digging sounds, a constant rhythm of pick hitting rock over and over again.

Duff started moving again and got all the way to the end of the drift, stopped and waited. He was about to turn when a gray fog, much less intense than the earlier black fog, came through the stone wall and hovered in front of them. Duff thought he saw the image of a face within the swirling fog, but it dissipated as quickly as it emerged.

"You guys see that?"

A concert of yesses filled the drift.

"The more it shows off, the less power it has. My senses tell me it's drained all of its energy by making these appearances. My guess is we won't encounter it again until it can save up more energy."

"I say we finish exploring all the drifts in the shaft and call it a day," Bowen suggested. "I could use more energy myself."

Together they explored the last drift at the end of the shaft, and then headed back to the main chamber. Cy had been drawing maps and documenting the shaft and drifts along the way, making notes where they encountered any paranormal activity and documenting what objects, if any, they stumbled upon during their exploration. They found little in the way of mining gear: a couple of picks, a rusted-out bucket, and an old lantern. But they did come across an empty Marlboro cigarette pack, stamped 1902, and one old leather boot.

The rest of the day was uneventful compared to the first part of the day, but by the time they made it back to the main chamber, they were all tired and hungry, and everyone seemed to have something significant on their mind. Bowen asked Lockey to take the lead as they climbed out of the mine. He wanted to be with Cy in the event he had any other encounters on his way up, but Cy climbed out of the mine right behind Lockey with Bowen and Duff right behind them and no incidents. An hour and a half later, they reached the Jeep, exhausted and hungry. It was going on four thirty, so they loaded their gear, drove to the nearest burger joint, and ordered beer and food. Bowen called the local authorities and told them they were out of the mine for the day and promised to call the next morning before they reentered.

"Well?" he said as he hit "end" on his cell phone and downed half of his beer. "Duff, can you explain what in the hell happened down there?"

Duff laughed. "Not really. This entity seems to have learned how to manifest itself in several different ways. That supposedly takes a long time to master, but from what little I could tell when it possessed me, I got the feeling it was fairly young when it died."

"It?" Lockey asked. "I got the distinct impression it was a man, a man struggling with something really big. I can't explain how, but his feelings mingled with mine, and I was overcome with his emotions. But what I felt most was pain and loneliness, mixed with guilt and anger. But the anger seemed to me to be the most prevalent."

"That's what scares me," Duff admitted. "He's made us all doubt ourselves and doubt who we are by reminding us of our faults and weaknesses. He's entered our dreams and created flashbacks and he's done it all with perfect aim."

"But what I want to know is how," Cy said. "How can he lock on to us at such a distance?"

"I don't know the answer to that, but I didn't get the feeling that *it*—" He paused and looked over at Lockey. "—or *he* was a strong entity. But he locked on to me even before we left New York. That has to be because of my abilities, but that takes strength and practice. Then

The Mystery of Ruby Lode

he locked on to all of you at different times, but after only one visit to the mine."

Bowen downed the last of his beer. "It seems so unreal that he knew how to push our buttons and make us doubt ourselves in such a short time."

"It's obvious to me now there are things in our pasts we've all struggled with, and some of those things still make us insecure. Which means no matter how much we think we've overcome certain aspects of our pasts, we've never really left them behind," Duff explained. "If he can zoom in on them that quickly, they are just under the surface and pretty strong within us."

"I never thought of it that way, and I never realized I was so insecure about my birth parents," Bowen confessed. "I really thought I was over all that, but I was obviously very wrong."

"Same here with the entire shoelace and restraint thing," Cy acknowledged. "As soon as we get back to the inn, I'm calling my parents and getting some answers."

"Guys," Duff warned, "he hit each one of our weaknesses and brought them to the forefront, making us second-guess who we are and how we live. He draws his strength from our weakness, and he'll continue to do so as long as we allow him to. Tonight, we talk all of this through."

Duff looked at Bowen. "First, we talk about you being given up for adoption and how you've felt about it and how it's affected you throughout your life." Then he looked at Cy. "After you talk to your parents and find out if any of that was true, we hash all that out as well." And lastly, he looked at Lockey. "You've obviously been bullied and teased and had socialization and abandonment issues as a kid, making friends and losing them, and these things have stuck with you into your adult life."

"Jeez, Duff, you make me sound like such a head case."

Cy and Bowen both looked at Lockey with surprised expressions. "Socialization and abandonment issues?" Cy joked. "Maybe I can see the abandonment issues because he can't keep a boyfriend, but socialization issues? Lockey's always the life of the party," he added.

"Apparently, I need therapy," Lockey whined.

Cy chuckled. "No one is debating that." Then they all laughed.

"But we'll get into all that later," Duff continued. "Which just leaves me. Well… well, we all know about my issues with Cy, but that's all out in the open now. More importantly, no offense, Cy, I've got to deal with my stepbrother abusing me. I've buried it way too long, and I didn't realize it still had such a hold on me."

Duff looked at each of them again. "Do you all understand where I'm going with this and why?"

"I think so," Lockey said. "If we talk all this out and bare our souls to each other, he can't come between us or use our weaknesses against us."

Duff smiled, looked around, then leaned over and kissed him. "Exactly! So let's enjoy our beer and burgers, get back to the inn so Cy can call his parents, we can all shower and get comfortable, then have a big old slumber party and share a little girl talk."

Chapter SEVEN

WHEN they got back to the inn, Cy and Bowen did exactly as planned. Cy showered first, and as usual, Bowen was there to hand him his towel. While Bowen showered, Cy called his parents. He dialed then hesitated before pressing the "send" button. *Could I have really been kidnapped? Is it possible to block out something like that for all these years? I guess I'll never know unless I ask.* He pressed "send."

The phone rang twice before his mother answered. "Hello?"

"Hey, Mom."

"Hey, honey. How is your vacation going?"

"'Very interesting' is one way to put it. But it's a very long story. I'll tell you all about it when we get back."

Cy's hands started shaking a little and his heart raced. *Here goes.*

"Mom, I have a really important question to ask you, and it's imperative you tell me the truth."

"Ooookay?"

"Uh, before we moved to Mississippi, was there something I was involved in that you kept from me?"

There was silence on the other end of the line. Cy heard a muffled sound, and he knew his mother was covering the phone and talking to someone, probably his father. His stomach dropped; in his heart he knew what the answer was. Cy rubbed his temple with his free hand. *Oh, my God, it's true. Okay, just hold it together long enough to get the details.*

"Cyrus, your father wants to talk to you."

Before he could answer her, she was no longer on the line.

"Hi, son." His dad sounded very nervous, and his voice cracked when he spoke.

"Hey, Dad."

"Your mother, uh… said you were inquiring about the time before we moved to Mississippi."

"Dad, I need to know the truth. Was I abducted?"

More silence. Then he heard his father cough and clear his throat before he said, "I would much rather talk about this in person."

"No, Dad, I need to know now. It's very important."

He heard his dad take a deep breath. *Here it comes.*

"Yes, son, you were abducted on your fifth birthday."

Cy turned his head away from the phone. "Damn." His knees started bouncing up and down and he felt very flushed. *Calm down, Cy. Jesus, how could I have blocked that out for so long?*

"Cyrus, are you there?"

"I'm here," he responded, not believing what he was hearing. "You're shitting me, right? You wouldn't have kept something like this from me for all these years?"

"Unfortunately, it's the truth, son. When we got you back, we took you to several psychiatrists and they all confirmed that you didn't remember a single detail. You'd blocked it all out somehow. The doctors said it was not uncommon for a child to push such a traumatic experience out of their mind to avoid dealing with it. Just as severe torture and pain can force a child to develop multiple personalities, fear can force you to push the experience so far back that sometimes it never surfaces. They said you may or may not ever remember, and they all advised us not to tell you and wait to see what happens."

Cy didn't know what to say, how to feel. He had been abducted, for Christ's sake. He stood and started pacing, but he didn't think his legs could hold him up, so he sat back down. "Tell me what happened, everything."

He heard his father sigh again. "Your mother had your fifth birthday party at the playground around the corner from our house in Islip, New York, on Long Island. There were about ten neighborhood kids there and some of their parents. I had to work and couldn't be there, but your Uncle Bob and Aunt Ellen helped your mother make everything special."

There was again silence on the phone. "Go on, Dad. It's okay."

"Is Bowen there with you?"

"He's in the shower, but, yes, he's here."

Cy heard his father sigh and then continue.

"Okay, so Uncle Bob was barbecuing and your Aunt Ellen and your mother, along with some of the other moms, were setting up the games. You kids were playing on the swings and merry-go-rounds. And, son, you have to understand, our neighborhood was very safe and nothing like this had ever happened before."

Cy interrupted him. "Dad, I don't blame you, but who did this to me and, more importantly, why?"

Silence again. "I'm getting to that, son. This is a pretty long story. Are you sure you don't want to wait until we can talk about this in person?"

"Dad, I need to know now and I can't explain why, but you'll just have to trust me."

"You know I trust you."

"It's important, Dad."

"I know, son. You won't remember this…."

Cyrus interrupted again. "I don't remember any of this."

"I'm sorry."

Cyrus took a deep breath and exhaled slowly. "No, I'm sorry, Dad. Go on."

"Anyway, when I was in the service, I flew transport planes for the Navy. I loved flying, so when I got out of the service, your mother and I married and flying was the only thing I knew how to do. I went to work for Alleghany Airlines flying the Long Island to Albany route out of MacArthur Airport in Islip. I was flying the day of your birthday party, as I explained earlier, and shortly before we started our approach into Albany, the cockpit door was kicked in. I was told we were being hijacked to a private landing strip in Ottawa, Canada. I had about thirty other passengers on board, and I wasn't about to allow anything to happen to them, so I refused and attempted to radio Albany. They stopped me by telling me they had you, and if I ever wanted to see you again, I would do as I was told."

Cy's stomach fell to his knees and he felt lightheaded yet again. Bowen walked out of the bathroom and when their eyes met, Cy was certain Bowen knew what was going on. His lover was at his side in an instant.

"Are you okay, son? Get Bowen."

"He's here now, Dad. Please go on."

"I'm sure you must know how that hit me like a ton of bricks. I didn't believe it at first, but right after they told me they had you, the airline put through an emergency call from the police explaining that you'd been abducted from the playground. Of course, at the time, the airline didn't know we were being hijacked and I couldn't tell them for fear of them hurting you. When I changed course for Ottawa, air traffic control notified me numerous times that I was off course. The kidnappers ordered me to break communications, but at the very last second, I told them we were being hijacked and the hijackers had my son. Of course there was nothing they could do until we landed, and they only had radar to track us. Once we touched down in Ottawa, the

The Mystery of Ruby Lode

hijackers gave me instructions as to where you could be found, and I relayed that to the authorities."

Cyrus had thousands of questions. He went over them in his head in an attempt to prioritize. "Dad, I need details about where I was taken and what was done to me."

"Cy, are you sure you want to know all this?"

"I have to know. I'm sure, Dad. Please just tell me, okay?"

His dad cleared his throat and started talking again. "Since the kidnappers were apprehended and charged, their attorney advised them to confess everything in an attempt to plea-bargain. We were later told your kidnappers were two very well dressed Portuguese men in their early thirties. They were working for the head of the Portuguese mafia, who was trying to flee the country and get back to Portugal before the authorities closed in on him. They took you from the playground, threw you in the backseat of the car, and drove to a quiet location where they stopped, then bound and gagged you, and put you in the trunk. They finally took you to an abandoned house on the coast in Montauk, and you were found, still bound and gagged, lying in a coat closet. We were also told that from the time you were abducted until the time you were rescued was just over six hours."

"Six hours," Cy mumbled. "Bound and gagged."

"Unfortunately, that answer is 'yes.' But when we got you back, you had no recollection of the ordeal. Your mother and I took you to several psychiatrists and… well, you know the rest."

Cy didn't realize it, but he'd been crying during most of the call. Bowen kept wiping his tears away and was there holding him and listening to every word through the phone.

"So how did we get to Mississippi?"

"The psychiatrists told us anything familiar could trigger your memory. If you went back to the playground, or if you saw something someone was wearing that reminded you of what the kidnappers were wearing, or even the scent of something could force you to remember. So the one thing we could do was to make sure you never saw that playground again, and the only way to do that was to move away. I quit Alleghany Airlines, and we packed up and moved the family to Mississippi."

"I can't believe all this happened to me" was the last thing Cyrus said before he dropped the phone.

"Son, are you there? Cyrus?"

Bowen picked up the phone. "Hey, Dad."

After Cyrus and Bowen had been together for a few years, and since Bowen had no real parents of his own, Cy's parents had insisted that Bowen call them Mom and Dad. They had always treated him like a son, and he loved them very much.

"Bo, is he all right?"

"Yeah, he's just a little shaken."

"Tell me what triggered this memory."

"A dream, Dad, a weird dream."

"Whatever it is that's going on, just please be careful."

"We will. Look, Dad, we've got a lot of information to sort through and it's kind of overwhelming. Can we call you guys when we get home?"

"I understand. Bo, tell Cyrus we are very sorry this has surfaced now. You know, Bo, parenting doesn't come with an instruction book, and all we could do was take the advice of the professionals and hope for the best."

"I'm sure he doesn't blame you guys. He knows deep down you did the best you could."

"Thanks, Bo. We'll talk to you in a few days."

Bowen pressed "end" on Cy's phone and dropped it on the bed. He wrapped his arms around Cy and held him tight. "Did you get the rest of that?"

"Yeah, most of it."

"I'm so sorry, Cy."

The Mystery of Ruby Lode

Cyrus felt Bowen's fingers running through his hair and caressing him gently, slowly. Through tears, he relayed the information to Bowen he'd missed while he was in the shower, and when he was through, they lay in silence, trying to process the ordeal. There was a light knock and a muffled voice from the other side of the adjoining door. "Okay for Lockey and me to come in?"

Cyrus wiped his eyes and they both stood. "Sure, come in, guys."

"Did you talk to your parents?" Duff inquired. But before Cy could respond, he saw his face and knew the answer.

Cy nodded. "My dream wasn't a dream at all. It was a flashback. That fucking spirit was tapping into something tucked away in the back of my memory since I was five years old."

"So it's true," Lockey said.

"Oh, it's true all right."

Cy told Duff and Lockey what his father had revealed during their call.

When Cy was through, Bowen took the lead. "Okay, it looks like we have some decisions to make as to how we proceed, if we decide to proceed."

Duff waved his hand. "What do you mean '*if* we proceed'? I've got to go back in there. This thing needs my help. I'm still not sure what we're dealing with, but either way, I've got to go back down there."

Lockey took Duff's hand in his. "He's right, guys. I felt it, and it's angry, no doubt. But at the same time, there was something else there. I got the sense it was very sad and alone behind all that anger. And as I said, for some reason, I sensed a great deal of guilt. It's okay if you guys want to call it a day, but I'm going back down there with Duff."

"Cy, it's up to you. Do you want to go home?"

Cy was now pacing back and forth like a caged tiger. "No! I want to see this through to the end. One for all and all for one, remember."

Duff smiled and squeezed Lockey's hand. They both held out their arms and Bowen and Cy stepped into a group hug.

Bowen was the first to break the embrace. Still wrapped in his towel, he stepped away and started digging through his suitcase for some clothes. "I've always wondered why the first people to explore Ruby Lode left without explanation, and well, I guess now I know." Looking at Duff, he asked. "Do you think that spirit has been there all along?"

"Probably," Duff answered. "Spirits don't usually stray very far from where they died. Some don't even know they're dead and others don't know how to cross over, so they wander aimlessly year after year until someone comes along and tries to help them. To answer your question, I'm sure if the other explorers entered Ruby Lode, they were scared away by our little friend."

"So what do we do?" Cy asked.

"I'm gonna go back down tomorrow. I need to try and get this guy to cross over."

Lockey raised his and Duff's joined hands in a show of support. "Me too, and I want to try and help."

Bowen looked at Cy with a questioning look. "You up to it?"

"If they're going back, I'm going back."

"And if you're going back, then I'm definitely going back," Bowen added.

Duff cleared his throat. "With that settled, we need to make sure the air is cleared between us."

"How so?" Cy asked.

"We can't go into Ruby Lode tomorrow with any secrets, grudges, or fears. If we do, the spirit will use that to its… I mean, to *his* advantage. United we stand, divided we fall is the best way I can explain it."

Cy was now pacing again. "You guys already know my little secret, and if truth be told, it wasn't even a secret. I didn't know a thing about it myself."

Bowen was slipping on the underwear, blue jeans, and T-shirt he'd dug out of his suitcase earlier. "You guys know my story now too. Being given up at birth had a much bigger emotional impact on me than I ever acknowledged, even to myself, and I think I'm gonna face it head on when we get home." He looked at Cy. "I've decided I'm going to try and find my birth parents. Who knows, maybe my mother was a knocked-up cheerleader and my father was a rapist, but maybe they weren't. Either way, the truth is something I can always deal with."

Cy nodded. "Whatever you decide, baby, I'll be right by your side."

"Guys, I don't think Lockey and I are going to be that easy. We both have some things to talk to you about."

"Besides having a woody for my husband?" Bowen asked with a coy smile.

Duff waved his hand. "Very funny."

"Uh, can I get dressed too?" Cy asked, digging in his suitcase. "Something about hearing dirty little secrets wearing nothing but a towel is a little creepy."

Lockey clapped his hands. "You guys are a laugh a minute, I tell ya."

"Oh, good, maybe we'll put together a comedy act," Cy said over his shoulder as he went into the bathroom.

Lockey walked over to the nightstand and picked up the phone. "I think I need some liquid courage."

He spoke into the phone. "Can you send two buckets of Corona and some limes up to the Telluride Room, please?"

When Lockey put down the phone, Duff reached over and took his hand. "It'll be okay. Lock, these guys are our best friends."

There was a knock on the door just as Cy was coming out of the bathroom.

Duff stood and headed to the door. He looked over his shoulder at Cy. "Took you long enough."

"Meaning?"

"Meaning we ordered beer, and it took you as long to get dressed as it took the beer to be delivered."

Cy's eyes lit up and he passed right over the ribbing. "You have beer?"

Duff rolled his eyes as he passed the bucket. "Yes, we have beer."

They each took one, slipped a wedge of lime down the long neck, and tapped their bottles together. Duff and Lockey kicked off their shoes and climbed up onto Cy and Bowen's king-size bed. Bowen followed and leaned against the headboard with Cy lying against his chest.

"You wanna go first, Lockey, or should I?"

Lockey exhaled nervously. "I'll go." He moved a little closer and Duff once again took his hand in a show of support.

"Look, guys, you probably won't see this as such a big deal, but it has haunted me for most of my life. I thought I'd come to terms with it, but Casper the ghost has made me realize I haven't done as good a job as I thought."

Duff squeezed his hand as Cy and Bowen looked on. "Look, I know you all think I'm the biggest stereotypical gay man who ever walked the earth, and I know why you think that. I live at the gym, I'm obsessed with the way I look, I go out all the time, I sleep around," he looked at Duff, "I used to sleep around, and for the most part, you're right about all that. But there are things that happened to me as a child that drive most of my wacky behavior."

Lockey downed his beer and wiped a bead of sweat off of his forehead with the back of his hand. He took a deep breath and let it out. "Okay, all you really know about my childhood is that I was a military brat that traveled around a lot. And that's true, but it's the effect that all that moving around had on me that's the problem."

Lockey painstakingly told the story he'd shared with Duff about leaving his friends and refusing to make new ones, becoming very withdrawn, gaining weight, and being bullied at school. Then he explained how, as an adolescent, he discovered the gym and how that discovery had turned his life around. He didn't need friends to work out. He'd lost weight, and slowly built his self-confidence. Then one day he came into his own and people stopped bullying him and started noticing him, in a good way. But eventually all that attention made him feel his entire self-worth was based on his good looks and muscular body, and if he were ever to lose either, he would go back to that lonely life he'd led as a child.

"Anyway, I know it's stupid. But that's what keeps me going to the gym, always looking my best, striving to be the life of the party, and always leaving them wanting more. I never got involved with any one guy because eventually, as with my childhood, he would leave me or I would be forced to leave him, and those scars, I can now see, still run pretty deep."

Lockey got up, handed everyone another beer and a wedge of lime, and got one for himself. "Well… aren't you going to tell me how stupid and shallow I am?"

Bowen looked down at Cy. "Not me," he said. "In fact, I think we owe you an apology. We took you at face value, no pun intended, and never looked for anything more."

"Speak for yourself," Cy said as he looked up at Bowen. "I always suspected there was something more to Lockey than met the eye, pun intended. But I never could figure him out. Lock, I always thought you had a thing for Duff, but you just kept on being the party guy and sleeping your way through New York, so I finally gave up on that idea."

"Yeah, Lock," Bowen added, "if you've always been so afraid of guys leaving you and relationships ending, what made you decide now was the time to take a chance on Duff?"

Lockey looked up at the ceiling. "I think it had something to do with the fact that wanting him and not having him had to be worse than having him and losing him. In the end, the result was the same, and at least I'd have him for a while. Besides, before Duff, I've never met anyone I thought was worth the risk."

Duff put his beer down and threw his arms around Lockey's neck. "That's the sweetest thing anyone has ever said about me. Thanks," he whispered then kissed him deeply.

Cy turned away with a mock look of disgust. "Good God, you two, get a room."

When the kiss ended, Lockey licked his lips, smiled, and looked at Bowen and Cy. "This guy is so worth the risk."

"OKAY, three down," Cy said. "Duff, that leaves you."

Duff got off of the bed and started pacing again. He thought about how to best start his story. He may have given them a hint as to what his brother had done to him, and shared a little more with Lockey, but he'd never told another soul the sordid details. And if the truth be told, he was nervous as hell about actually saying the words out loud. He took a deep breath and swallowed hard. *Here goes!*

"Guys, my story is twofold. You already know my mother and sister died during childbirth and my father married a woman with four teenage boys shortly thereafter, but what you don't know is...." Duff stopped pacing, looked at Lockey, and was rewarded with the reassurance he so desperately needed in the form of a nod and a smile.

Duff explained how he didn't fit in well with his new family and how his stepbrothers had all picked on him continuously. He also told them he realized if he stuck to himself and never asked for anything and stayed out of everyone's way, most of them would leave him alone. He confided that self-preservation had kicked in and he literally became invisible in his own home. He remembered the only thing he had was school, and he focused on that and his grades were excellent because of it.

As he thought back, he tried to hold the tears at bay. "And that's the time in my life when something within me fundamentally changed and I lost all of my self-confidence. I became shy and reserved, and, no matter how hard I tried, I've just never been able to overcome it."

The Mystery of Ruby Lode

"I had no idea, Duff," Cy offered. "That must have really sucked."

"Where was your father during all of this?" Bowen asked.

"He was around. He was into his new wife. His new stepsons were older and into sports, so they quickly formed a bond and had a great little family. I just wasn't part of it." Duff wiped a tear from his cheek. He opened another beer and passed the bucket around again.

Bowen slipped away from Cy and gave Duff a hug. "That must have been tough for an eight-year-old boy. I'm really sorry."

"Thanks, Bo, but I'm not finished."

Bowen stepped back from Duff and looked him in the eye. "There's more?"

"Unfortunately, yes, there's so much more."

Duff broke the embrace and walked over to the window and stared off into the distance. Out of the corner of his eye, he caught movement and turned to see Bowen back on the bed, quickly wrapped in Cy's embrace. He again turned to the window as if all the courage he needed was just on the other side of the windowpane. He was brought back to reality by Lockey's arms surrounding him. He dipped his head just a little when Lockey kissed him on the neck and whispered words of encouragement into his ear. "It's okay, Duff. I'm here and I'm not going anywhere."

Duff turned, kissed Lockey, and led him back to the bed where he took his seat. *And now for the tough part.* "Okay, when I told you if I didn't ask for anything and minded my own business, most of my stepbrothers left me alone, that was true. Most of them did, but not all of them. My fourteen-year-old stepbrother Abe was pissed off he drew the short straw and had to share a room with me, and he gave me hell from the moment he moved in. He was a teenaged baseball jock, brought all his trophies and banners, then took over my entire room, but because he was also the oldest, he thought he had every right to do it. He also resented the fact he was always forced to babysit me when my parents were out and tortured the hell out of me every time he had to miss something he wanted to do because he had to babysit me. That's when I got it the worst. At first, it was just stupid stuff like ripping the sheets off of my bed just after I made it, or throwing my toothbrush in the toilet.

"He had these prized miniature wooden baseball bat trophies for hitting the most number of home runs in a season, and once I made the mistake of touching one of them. He beat the hell out of me with that little wooden bat, leaving knots on my head for weeks. And that's when he started getting physical, slapping and kicking me when the door was closed and throwing me on the bed and shoving my face into the pillow until I would just about pass out from lack of oxygen. Then one night my life changed forever."

Duff stopped to gain his composure and forced himself to get this out without breaking down.

"One night, my dad and stepmother were out and I don't know where my other stepbrothers were, but it was just Abe and me at home. He pulled the usual and slapped me around a few times, nothing new. And then threw me on the bed, facedown with my face in the pillow, trying to suffocate me. Again nothing new. I'd been through it a million times and knew the drill. In fact, I learned that sometimes if I pretended to pass out quickly, he would leave me alone." Duff chuckled through tears. "I guess that's where I learned to be a survivor. But this time in particular, instead of forcing my face into the pillow, he lay down on top of me. I felt something hard pressing against my back. I was only eight. I had no idea what an erection was, but as he dry humped my ass, fear ripped through me, and the next thing I knew, he was ripping my pants off. I heard him spit and I felt something warm and slick at my backside, and then all I remember is gut-wrenching pain."

Duff could hardly take remembering all of this. Somehow talking about it made all the pain come back. He dropped onto the bed and covered his face with his hands. Within seconds, he felt Lockey's arms wrap tightly around him, and he buried his face into the chest of the warm, supportive man embracing him. It must have been the combination of the adrenaline rush, finally telling someone his story, and having Lockey there to hold and protect him that triggered something because he cried like he'd never cried before. It was uncontrollable. The gut-wrenching sobs seemed to last forever. He wanted to stop, but he just couldn't. Lockey simply held him close.

Bowen looked up at Cy through teary eyes. "Oh, my God, baby, how could we not have known this?"

Cy wiped the tears from his own eyes and just shook his head. "I don't know, but I can't imagine what it must have been like for him. He must have felt so alone, and with no one to turn to, I don't know how he survived. All I know is, if his father wasn't already dead, I'd kill him for emotionally and physically abandoning his own son."

When Duff was able to compose himself, he attempted to finish his story. Duff cleared his throat. "I… I must have passed out, because when I woke up, there was blood all over me and my sheets and Abe was standing over me, very nervous, like he thought he must have killed me. He made me take a shower, wash my linens, and again told me if I ever told anyone what he'd done, he would kill me."

Duff looked down at the floor again. "And this went on a couple times a week for the next couple of years," he admitted in a hushed tone. "Slowly, over the next year and a half, I started to fill out and gain a little weight. I had no idea why, but I promised myself when I turned ten years old, I was going to put a stop to it. I don't know why ten was such a significant number, but I was a kid, and I think it was a subconscious goal I gave myself just to be able to get through it all somehow.

"On my tenth birthday, it all came to an end. My dad and stepmother went to one of my stepbrother's football games, leaving Abe and me home alone. Abe had figured out that using some kind of hand lotion felt better and would apply it liberally to me and himself while I was face down in the pillow. For the first time in two years, I asked to be on my back. Abe gave me a questioning look but just smiled. I guess he thought I was starting to enjoy it, and maybe he was in a giving mood that night or something, because he nodded. As I lay on my back watching him playing with himself, spreading lotion on his dick, I knew it was now or never."

Duff kissed Lockey's forehead, released his hand and got up and moved to the window again. After a couple of minutes, he turned and faced them with a slight smile. "When he was done lubricating himself, he pushed my knees against my chest and knelt over me, legs spread, smiling. This time, I, too, smiled and before he knew what hit him, with all my strength, I heel butted him in the balls with my right foot. Instinctively, his hands went to his groin, and then I kicked him in the head with the other foot. He rolled off of the bed and hit the floor. But I wasn't through with him. As he lay there on his arms and knees, hands covering his groin, I reached up and grabbed that same wooden baseball bat he'd beaten me with, rubbed a little lotion on it, and shoved it up his ass as hard as I could. He cried out in pain, and all I could do was smile. He started to cry and begged me to pull it out, so I did and rammed it back in a second time, and a third. He finally fell to his side and took the fetal position. I left the bat up his ass, kicked him in the head, and I grabbed him by the hair and forced him to look at me. I'll never forget this part as long as I live. I looked him directly in the eye as I squeezed his cheeks. 'If you ever so much as touch me again, *I will kill you.* I'll wait for you to go to sleep and I'll beat you to fucking death with your own baseball bat and not the little one still stuck up your ass. You got it? No one, including you, will ever touch me there ever again.'

"I saw the pain and humiliation in his eyes, and it was one of the happiest days of my life."

"That's my boy," Lockey said. "I'm so proud of you. Did he ever touch you again?"

"Never! Nor has anyone else for that matter. A couple of years later, he joined the army, and I never saw him again. Because my grades were so good, as you well know, I eventually went to NYU on a full scholarship and never looked back. My dad died of a massive heart attack the spring I turned eighteen, and my stepmom and I tolerated one another until I went off to NYU in the fall. I've never spoken to any of them since the day I walked out of that house. I received a check from my father's estate a year later, and that's what I lived on during college.

I got another check for my portion of the proceeds from the house when my stepmother died. And that was the end of that."

"We had no idea," Cy offered tenderly.

"Of course you didn't. I never gave you any indications."

"I mean, we knew you didn't associate with your family, but that's not quite that uncommon. But to be raped continually by your stepbrother, that's a whole other element I didn't see coming. I don't know what to say."

"There is nothing you can say. But you know... I've gotta tell you, somehow sharing this with you guys has liberated me a little, I think. I feel like I've sort of been living under a rock and just crawled out for the first time. Now I can start to leave the weight of that rock behind."

Bowen and Cy crawled off of the bed and approached Duff with open arms. Lockey joined them, and they shared another group hug.

Duff was the first to step back. "Guys, let's not forget why we got into all of this in the first place. We can't have any more secrets between us, so if there is anything else we need to divulge, we need to do it now. And Cy and Bowen, that includes any secret between the two of you. I'm not going to pry, but if either one of you has kept something significant from the other, you come clean or you stay the hell out of that mine. You can do it in the privacy of your own room, but you need to do it one way or the other. If you don't, I guarantee it will all come out tomorrow one way or the other."

Cy looked at Bowen and took his hand. "I'm good."

"I'm good too," Bowen assured them.

Duff, Bowen, and Cy all looked at Lockey. Lockey threw his hands up in the air. "Whattt?" he whined. "I'm good too. You all know how shallow I am. There's not enough room in here for more than a couple of secrets."

They all laughed.

Duff stifled a yawn. "Okay, on that note, I'm gonna turn in. I'm emotionally drained and I have a feeling tomorrow is going to be a very interesting day."

"I'm with you," Lockey said as he took Duff's hand and led him to their room.

Duff stopped and ran back and hugged Cy and Bowen again. "Thanks, guys, I love you both."

"Ditto," Cy whispered.

"Love you," Bowen added.

Duff headed for the door. "Good night, guys."

Chapter EIGHT

CY CLOSED the door between the adjoining rooms and looked at Bowen. "Can you believe what Duff had to endure all those years ago?"

"I can't imagine the hell. God, that must have been tough."

"Isn't it odd that each one of us has had something in our past we thought we'd dealt with, but in all actuality haven't been able to let go of?"

"I guess," Bowen conceded. "But I think a lot of people have things in their past they thought they'd dealt with but creeps back into their lives at some time or another. I'll give you this; it is strange that our issues collectively—abandonment, abduction, abuse, and bullying—are all things that are still prevalent in our society today and things we see on the daily news."

"I never thought about it that way, but you're right. Abduction—God, I still can't believe I was kidnapped as a child. That's the kind of thing that happens to other people, not me, and to have blocked it out for all these years...." Cy felt a chill run up his spine and he wrapped his arms around himself.

"Come here, baby," Bowen urged as he crossed their room. When they met, Bowen rubbed his hands up and down Cy's shoulders and arms. The caress reassured Cy that Bowen was there for him in every way. "I want you, Bo. I need to feel connected to you, to be inside of you," he whispered.

"I'm here, baby, now and always."

Their lips met in a passionate kiss that instantly deepened into a desperate need to be naked. Cy pushed Bowen toward the bed as he pulled his T-shirt over his head. He unbuttoned Bowen's pants and forced them down to his ankles. Bowen pulled his own T-shirt over his head and tossed it across the room as Cy ravished his lips and neck. When they reached the bed, they fell, Cy on top of Bowen, never breaking their embrace. He broke away from the kiss just long enough to slide down to the foot of the bed, taking Bo's underwear with him and slipping them off along with his jeans. He unbuttoned his own jeans and stepped out of them, never breaking eye contact with his lover.

He slipped his underwear off and climbed back on top of Bowen. When their lips met again, it was like electricity was flowing through them both. After ten years, the spark, the excitement, and the need were all still there, and right now they were working on overload. Bowen's hands caressing his back felt like leather and silk all at once and the feeling instantly sent chills up and down his spine. Bo's unique smell consumed his senses, and at that very moment in time, smelling Bowen, tasting him, wanting him, and needing him were all that mattered. Feeling the love flowing between them overloaded every nerve ending in his body, and he was electrified. Over the years, they had slowly peeled away the other's many layers, and now when they made love, it was soft, pure, raw, and desperate all rolled into one.

Bowen wrapped his legs around Cy's midsection and brought their raging erections together in a dance they both knew all too well. As they kissed, their dicks touched lightly, ground forcefully, then teased mercilessly until they were both already leaking, the overture for what was to come. He lifted Bowen off of the bed, never breaking their frantic kiss, and walked into the bathroom. He set Bowen down on the bathroom counter as he anxiously searched his shaving kit. He was so thankful to be in a committed, monogamous relationship, which allowed them to forego condoms, but the lube they didn't want to do without. With the container in hand, he was about to lift Bowen again, but looking in the mirror, he couldn't help but stare at the way Bowen's muscles flexed when he moved. Each time their dicks met, his body would completely tense and then he relaxed into the sensation. *God, I'll never get used to looking at this man.*

"I love you, Bo."

"Love you more."

He effortlessly lifted Bowen off of the counter and carried him back to the bed. Somewhere along the line they'd relaxed and the pace changed from frantic and desperate to soft and tender lovemaking. He gently lowered Bowen again and broke their kiss as he slid down and took him into his mouth. He heard Bowen gasp as his lips encircled the man he loved and could never live without. He could already taste Bowen's excitement, and in the beginning, that taste had always been enough to just about push him over the edge. But through experience and time, he'd learned to control his desires and take his time to pleasure Bowen as long as he could.

He allowed Bowen to slide from his mouth as he slipped down farther and took his balls and consumed them. Again, his senses were filled with Bowen's own unique musk, and as he jostled Bowen's balls in his mouth, his nose was in a prime location to inhale his wonderful scent. With each breath, his dick got harder until he didn't know how much longer he could hold on. He moved down farther still and ran his tongue over the ultrasensitive area surrounding Bowen's opening. The soft, almost silken skin flexed with anticipation as Cy tantalized it with his tongue. Bowen pulled his legs back and spread his ass cheeks to give Cy more access. When Cy's tongue breeched Bowen's opening, he was rewarded with moan after moan as Bowen wiggled his tight little ass in his face. His anticipation was growing rapidly along with his erection, and he knew he couldn't hold out much longer. He pulled back and opened the lube, squeezing some onto his finger, spreading it around Bo's waiting hole. He probed inside, which brought more moans of pleasure from Bowen—one finger, then two, and then slowly three before Bowen was about ready. As Bowen gyrated on his fingers, Cy prepared him for the invasion soon to follow. He stood at the foot of the bed and pulled Bowen's legs over his shoulders. He looked down at the man trusting and loving him. "God, you're beautiful."

"I love you, Cyrus Curran."

He smiled and positioned himself at Bowen's opening. Bowen placed his hands on Cy's thighs to help guide him along, and he followed the lead. As he pushed in little by little, Bowen controlled his entry, signaling him to pause now and then to allow Bowen time to relax and accept the foray. But within seconds Cy was buried deep within his lover, getting the connection he so desperately needed. He took Bowen's legs by the ankles and lifted them off of his shoulders and held them straight in the air. He started to move in and out, slowly at first, then a little faster, pulling almost all the way out and then sliding back in as far as his length would allow. With each stroke, his nerve endings became alive and lit on fire. He placed Bowen's feet against his chest and continued the assault until they were both moaning with pleasure. "I need you so much, Bo," he said through gasping breaths.

"I need you, too, baby, you feel so good inside me. Keep fucking me."

He loved how they were always so very open in their lovemaking and how they often changed positions from top to bottom and back to top. But he'd noticed over the years that who topped or bottomed always seemed to have something to do with what was going on in their lives at the time. One of them may have had a bad week and just needed to give up control and be taken care of, or one of them needed a little extra reassurance or that connection he needed now. But either way, neither of them was hung up on who was supposed to be the top or bottom like some other couples they knew. They both allowed the other to be who they were and to need what they needed, and it had always worked for them. Each always seemed to know what the other needed, and both of them were willing to fulfill that need.

Cy looked down and watched with great anticipation as his dick slipped in and out of Bowen, a sight he never got tired of and that turned him on to no end. He squeezed more lube onto his hand and started to fondle Bowen's dick in unison with his slow, gentle thrusts. Bowen's hands covered his and set the pace. "I'm so close, babe."

"Me too."

Cy moaned and was soon plunging in and out, with Bowen pulling him in as far as he could with each powerful thrust. He felt his release building deep within his core and knew the explosion was near. He dropped Bowen's feet from his chest and felt Bowen lock them behind his back as he leaned over and kissed him passionately. He whimpered into Bowen's mouth as his heart raced, his balls drew up tight, and he shot his first spurt deep inside his lover. He straightened and took Bowen's dick into his hand and stroked it as he released string after string into his lover's warm gut. He felt Bowen tighten around him and heard the familiar sound of his lover about to let go. He plunged in and out, deeper and faster, as Bowen shot, his first load landing on his own bottom lip and chin. He continued plunging in and out as the next two rounds landed on Bowen's neck and chest respectively. He kept up the thrusts until he was empty and Bowen had milked himself dry, and then he collapsed. When he was able to catch his breath, he looked at Bowen, who was slowly sliding his legs from around his waist. When he slipped from Bowen's warmth, he saw him flinch just a little.

Cy smiled teasingly. "You are quite a sight."

Bowen chuckled as he rolled to face him. "How about helping a guy clean a little of this up?"

"My pleasure," Cy said as he licked Bowen's essence from his lips and chin and then kissed him deeply.

"Yum," Bowen said, as he tasted himself on Cy's tongue. "I'm good. Real good."

Cy laughed as he got up and went to the bathroom to get a warm cloth, then slowly and sensually cleaned Bowen's face, neck, and chest. He flipped the towel over and cleaned them both before lying down next to him.

Cy snuggled into Bowen's waiting arms. "Do you know how much I love you?"

Bowen pretended he was pondering the question. "I think I have an idea, but I still love you more."

Cy smiled a contented smile. "Then that gives me something to strive for."

He heard Bowen's chuckle and felt him tighten his hold while placing a gentle kiss on his shoulder. He wrapped Bowen's arms tightly around his chest, bringing one hand to his lips as he kissed each finger one by one. He nestled Bowen's hand under his chin, closed his eyes, and tried to sleep.

He listened to the slow, even breaths as Bowen drifted off to sleep and thought about his abduction. Despite all the unanswered questions, he couldn't be anything but happy. He was living the life he was supposed to be living, and doing it with the person he was meant to be with. Whatever happened to him as a child surely affected him, but it wouldn't break him, and he certainly wasn't going to give the abductors the power to affect his happiness. He buried his nose in the bend of Bowen's arm and breathed in his scent as he drifted off to sleep.

VERY early the next morning, it was still dark as they drove through the golden arches and got breakfast sandwiches on the way to the mine. While they ate, Duff noticed everyone was exceptionally quiet. None of the regular banter and endless teasing filled the Jeep, and it made him the least bit uneasy. After thinking about it briefly, he realized he craved the normalcy of their stupid antics. It was something he could count on no matter what, something to ground him.

But as his mind wandered, he understood their reserve. He, too, was worried about what they would find, but he could see and sense things they couldn't and that made him feel better off somehow. Everything they were dealing with was new territory and he, above anyone, could understand how the unknown can be very scary. His mind drifted back to the first time he saw a spirit. He was in the backyard playing, and his mother, pregnant with his baby sister at the time, was working in her garden. This lady ran up to him and threw her arms around him, but her arms kept going right though him. He remembered being frightened, not because she was scary looking, but because he could see right through her. She was smiling and seemed so happy to have found him, but she'd had the saddest eyes he'd ever seen. The confused look on her face had stayed with him for many years, and it took him just that many to understand why.

Suddenly, his mother was standing beside him, scooping him up in her arms. "No! I'm sorry, this is not your son, this is my son," his mother had told the woman.

The lady's expression turned from one of joy to pain and sadness.

"Your son is in the light. Cross over into the light and he'll be waiting for you," she'd added. The lady looked over her shoulder, then back at his mother. His mother nodded. "Yes, go into the light. He'll be there, I promise you." The lady smiled, reluctantly turned, and walked away, disappearing into thin air.

His mother had explained to him in terms a five-year-old could understand that she was looking for her son who had been taken from her but unfortunately was no longer alive. She explained she'd missed her son so much she'd taken her own life. But she didn't realize her son was no longer alive, so she didn't want to leave this plane without him. She also explained that sometimes people would come to people like them when they needed their help, and he must help them just like she had helped the sad lady today. She'd made him promise to never turn anyone away that needed the use of his gift.

"Dufffff!" Cy huffed.

"Whaaaaat?"

"Earth to Duff! I've been talking to you for the last two minutes."

"I'm sorry. I was zoning out."

"I can tell. Do you wanna share?"

"Nah, it was nothing."

Lockey grabbed his hand. "Are you okay, baby?"

"Yeah, thanks. I was just thinking about my mother."

Everyone went silent.

Duff looked around the Jeep. "Well, now that you have my attention, talk."

Cy turned around from the front seat. "We were just wondering if there is anything we can do to try and prepare ourselves mentally for what we're gonna find down there. I mean, we have no more secrets between us, so it can't hurt us in that way, but can you tell us what we should expect?"

Duff thought for a few seconds. "It's really hard to say, guys. I wish it was black and white, but it's just not that simple."

"We figured as much. We just thought we'd ask."

"What I can tell you," Duff explained, "is that this thing gets its energy from our fear and it will do everything in its power to suck us dry. It will start tapping into our energy the second it senses our presence."

Lockey shivered. "Can we do anything to block it?"

"Not without a lot of practice, and we don't have the time for that. The best you can do is try not to be afraid. And if you are afraid, do your best not to show it."

The Jeep was abruptly quiet again.

"Look, guys, I'm perfectly capable and willing to go down there alone. This is my mission in life, not yours."

"Absolutely not," Lockey protested.

The Mystery of Ruby Lode

Bowen, who was driving and had been totally quiet up until then, suddenly had a voice. "We're in this together, for better or worse."

"Yeah," Cy agreed. "All for one and one for all, remember?"

Bowen lifted his fist in the air and they all did another knuckle bump.

"I'm sorry to drag you into this with me. It's just...." Duff's voice trailed off and started to crack. "It's just, I made a promise to my mother that I would never turn anyone away who needed my help, and I need to keep my promise."

Lockey kissed Duff's cheek. "And we're gonna help you do it, baby."

Cy turned around in his seat again and looked Duff in the eye. "I say we go and drop-kick some spirit ass all the way to the other side."

That was met with a chorus of "Hell yeah!" and "Let's do it."

For the first time since his mother died, Duff finally felt like he had a family again. "You guys are the best."

BOWEN pulled the Jeep up to the base of the mountain as the sun was just starting to peek over the ridge. They again unloaded their gear, suited up, and ran through the all-too-familiar safety check. They started up the mountain in single file with Duff taking the lead, hoping to sense any surprises that might come their way. With adrenaline pumping through his veins, Duff maneuvered the last hundred yards and threw down the line to make it a little easier for the others. Once everyone was at the mine, Bowen rechecked everyone's gear and placed a call to the local authorities, as he'd done the day before, to let them know their plans. When he ended his call, the four of them stood looking at the mine's opening. No one said a word, but everyone knew what the others were thinking. The time had come to test their abilities and, more importantly, the strength of their friendship. This was a defining moment in all of their lives, and each of them could tell the others were uneasy—for different reasons, of course, but uneasy just the same. Bowen raised his palm and they followed suit and high-fived each other, again without saying a word.

Duff was the first one down the main shaft, taking his time, constantly looking over his shoulder. When he was through the tightest part of the shaft, the part where Cy got stuck, he stopped. He sensed he was no longer alone in the small tunnel and waited to see if he could pick up more. "He's here, guys," he yelled up to the opening.

Lockey yelled back down, "Are you okay?"

"Yeah, I'm just going to hang for a few to see if I can pick up anything else."

"We can have you back up in a flash if we need to. Just say the word."

"Roger that."

Duff stood frozen with feet spread and firmly planted on the age-old wall of the mineshaft. Holding on firmly to the rappelling line wrapped around his waist, he tried to slow his heart rate and open his mind. He could sense the spirit's presence, but he could get no more. In order to help the spirit cross over, it needed to want to be helped. That meant knowing it was dead and knowing it should move on, but he sensed the spirit knew neither.

Continuing down to the chamber, he looked over his shoulder and saw a brief flash of light, but it was quickly gone. "Go ahead, flex your muscles. If this is the way you want it to go down, I'll bite and play the game!"

Duff continued until he hit the floor of the small chamber below. "I'm down," he yelled as he released the line.

"I'm next," Lockey yelled down the shaft.

"Okay, just take your time."

When Duff turned around to investigate the source of the light, he gasped when he was greeted with a faceless head formed out of thick black fog, but nothing in the form of a body was attached. He sensed

The Mystery of Ruby Lode

some sadness and regret, but the entity was mostly consumed with anger. Duff turned away when he heard Lockey yell that he was almost there. When he looked back, the entity was gone.

Damn!

Lockey dropped down into the chamber, and Duff helped him with his harness. Once free of the rappelling gear, he yelled up the shaft, signaling it was okay for Cy to start his descent.

When Lockey turned around, Duff felt his glare. "Okay, what happened? And don't tell me nothing happened because I know better."

Knowing he was busted, Duff sighed. "I had a visitor. But... I'd rather tell all of you at once, if you don't mind."

"Okay, I'll wait, but remember, we promised no more secrets."

"I swear I wasn't going to keep this from you. I just wanted to tell everyone at the same time."

"Okay, I believe you." Lockey stepped up to Duff and kissed him tenderly. Suddenly there was a deep, guttural roar that ran through the shaft. They both froze and heard Cy, halfway down, yell, "What in the hell was that?"

Duff yelled, "We've got company, but come on down. Everything's okay."

Cy dropped into the chamber a few minutes later, unhooked, and signaled for Bowen to start his descent. While they waited for Bowen, Duff paced in the small chamber as Lockey explained to Cy that Duff had been visited earlier.

Minutes later Bowen was down and they were once again together.

Lockey put his hands on his hips. "Okay, Duff, we're all here. Tell us what happened."

Duff filled them in on what he'd experienced with the entity, and Cy explained to Bowen about the horrible roar.

"Okay, guys," Duff urged, "let's not let this spook us, no pun intended. We need to keep our heads together so I can see if I can help this spirit cross over."

"What now?" Lockey asked.

"We explore the second shaft. I feel like that's where the energy source is located and where we'll find our spirit."

THE guys checked their gear again, and each turned on the flashlight on their helmet along with the one hanging on their belts. Everything was in good working order, so they were all ready to go.

"What do you say we follow the same plan as yesterday?" Bowen suggested. "We can work our way to the end of the shaft and explore each drift on our way back to the chamber. Does everyone agree?"

Duff stepped forward. "Yep, but I'll take the lead. That way I might be able to stop any onslaught of spiritual activity before it gets to you."

Cy and Bowen jokingly pushed him toward the shaft's opening and stood behind him. "Okay by us," they said, looking at each other and smiling.

"Very funny, you guys." He stuck his hand in Lockey's direction. "Let's go, babe. We'll leave these sissies here."

Lockey stood in line behind Cy and Bowen and stuck his head around them to look at Duff. "You too?" Duff laughed.

"Nah, I'm just kidding. I'm with you." He made his way to the head of the line to join Duff, and they entered the shaft.

This was obviously the most recently mined shaft because there were rails on the ground and a few ore carts blocking the entry to the first drift on the left, as well as lanterns, picks, and chisels left behind by who knows how many miners. They pushed farther into the shaft, and Duff stopped when he heard a faint rumble. It was slowly getting louder and louder. "Shhhh, do you hear that?"

The Mystery of Ruby Lode

The others stopped and listened. "Yeah," Bowen said. "It sounds like metal against metal."

With each second, the noise grew louder and it seemed like the source of the sound was getting closer and closer still.

"Ore cart," Duff yelled. "Get to the side of the shaft. Now!"

Everyone jumped to the outsides of the iron rails under their feet and hugged the walls of the shaft. No sooner was everyone out of the way when an ore cart full of rocks came barreling around the bend in the shaft, headed right for them. "Back," Bowen yelled as the cart flew past them. It slowed when it ran out of rail at the mouth of the shaft, but stopped at the opposite end of the chamber. The impact made a huge sound and the entire mine shook.

"Back to the chamber!" Bowen yelled as he took Cy by the hand and pulled him out of the shaft. Lockey did the same to Duff, and they met and stood in the center of the chamber, waiting to see if any one of the three shafts might collapse.

Everything settled down and all was quiet again.

Bowen shined his flashlight around the chamber. "Duff, what do you think?"

"It's just trying to scare us. It doesn't want us down here, but what I can't tell you is why."

Duff watched the glow of Bowen's flashlight as it moved over the walls. "What do you think about the shaft? Think it's safe?"

Bowen shrugged his shoulders. "More importantly, are you sensing any danger?"

"Of course I'm sensing danger, you idiot. We're in an abandoned mine with an angry ghost."

"I meant about the mine, you ass. Any premonitions?"

"My senses are on overload, and I can't really tell. We'll just have to take our chances."

"I say we go," Cy suggested. They all looked at each other and nodded.

They again entered the shaft and proceeded slowly, listening for any surprises. They rounded the first bend and walked right into a dead end. "This can't be right," Cy said as he dug in his backpack for the early sketches he'd discovered while researching the mineshaft. "This shaft should have gone on for at least another sixty yards with—" He counted. "—eight more drifts." While Cy and Bowen studied the sketch, Lockey leaned against the wall and fell right through it, landing on his ass. They all stared in amazement as he looked up with a surprised look on his face.

Duff offered a hand to Lockey, who was still sitting on the ground in semi-shock. He accepted and Duff pulled him to his feet.

Duff started his favorite pastime and paced back and forth. "The whole thing was an illusion," he mumbled. "The minute Lockey fell through it, the wall disappeared. It looks to me like he really doesn't want us to go any farther into the shaft."

Duff kicked the ground in anger. "This thing is starting to royally piss me off. Let's go!"

He took off down the shaft when Lockey grabbed his arm. "Stop! Take a deep breath and think about what you're doing."

"He's right," Cy warned. "You can't go barreling off down that shaft when you have no idea what's waiting for you at the other end."

Duff pulled his arm away from Lockey's grip and paced some more. "I feel so fucking frustrated," he mumbled. "If I knew what it wanted or why it's trying to keep us from the shaft, I could do something, but these tricks… these tricks make me feel so fucking helpless."

"Duff, shake it off. This isn't your fault," Cy said. "We all came along of our own free will, not just here, but on this entire trip. Who knew we were going to encounter something like this?"

Cy took Duff into an embrace. "It's okay," he whispered in his ear. "We're all okay." He kissed Duff's cheek. "Now let's go and see what we can find."

The Mystery of Ruby Lode

Lockey touched Cy's arm and mouthed "thank you" as Cy picked up his backpack and threw it over his shoulder. Cy gave him a quick wink and off they went.

They passed two more drifts, one on the left and one on the right, with no abnormal activity, but as they approached the next drift, a draft started to form, which turned into a breeze and then into wind. Suddenly they were being pushed back two steps for every one step forward. As the wind blew past them, threatening to knock them down, Duff yelled, "Link your arms together and grip your forearms tightly."

They all struggled to do as Duff explained and soon they were pushing ahead through the narrow shaft, barely able to fit four across but managing. Duff thought they must have looked like characters from the Wizard of Oz following the yellow brick road. As they made their way against the force of the wind, it started to die down, little by little. First to a breeze, then a draft, until it finally stopped.

They released their arms, pushed down their hair—which was totally standing on end, except for Bowen's, which was so short it didn't move—and tried to catch their breath.

"This thing really doesn't want us to get any farther," Duff said. "But why?"

They started their journey again, and as they passed two more drifts, they were on their toes waiting for anything out of the ordinary. Suddenly, Duff's next step squished under his boot. His next step squished even louder. *What the fuck?* "Guys, stop."

Think, Duff! Oh, no. "Bat shit!" he mumbled. But before he had time to explain, he heard a loud rumble and yelled, "Bats, everybody down!"

Duff dove for the ground and felt Lockey on top of him as the bats passed inches above their heads. There must have been thousands of them, and it took a good three minutes for the onslaught to end. When Duff looked over, Cy was on top of Bowen and there was a bat stuck in his hair. He was beating himself to death trying to get it out.

Duff started laughing uncontrollably, and as soon as Lockey saw what was going on, he started laughing as well. Poor little Bowen was still stuck under Cy's six-foot-six-inch frame and had no idea what the hell was happening.

Before Duff or Lockey could get to Cy, they watched him rip the little bat out with a hunk of hair and throw it against the wall.

"I'm glad you think that's funny," Cy snapped as he rubbed his head.

He rolled off of Bowen, who was completely covered in bat shit, which only made them laugh harder. Cy saw Bowen, forgot about his bat incident, and started laughing right along with his buddies. Bowen eventually had to smile as well, and they all had a much-needed break in the tension. They were laughing so hard they didn't see what was creeping up behind them. Duff caught movement out of the corner of his eye, and when he turned, he saw the black fog hovering above them. "Guys, don't look now, but we have company."

The laughter quickly faded when the others looked up and saw what Duff had seen earlier. This time the fog had no head but floated above them like a cloak. Suddenly, deep within the darkness of the cloak, Duff saw himself as a child face down in his bed with his stepbrother on top of him. His first reaction was to turn and run, but he couldn't let the spirit win. Anger built within him.

"Is that all you got? You're gonna have to do better than that." He stood and crossed his arms over his chest. He turned and the others were all frozen, staring up at the fog unable to move. The fog began to dissipate and was suddenly gone.

Cy started rubbing his head again. "What in the hell was that all about?"

"It's trying to rattle us, is all."

"I think it's working," Cy mumbled.

"Like hell it is," Duff said matter-of-factly. "I'm done with this shit. Let's get this show on the road."

Duff watched as Bowen tried to get as much of the bat shit off of him as he could while Cy continued rubbing his head.

Lockey was beside him instantly. "Was that you and your brother?"

"Yeah."

"But how could it know that?"

"It's projecting straight from my memory."

"I'm really sorry, baby. That couldn't have been easy to see."

"No need to be sorry. It was part of my past, and I somehow feel so liberated that it's out and everyone knows. I have half a mind to bring charges against my fucking stepbrother when I get back to New York."

"Whatever you decide, you know I'll be right there with you."

Duff kissed Lockey tenderly, and again that horrible roar emanated from deep within the mine.

"What the hell?"

Lockey looked around the shaft with his head cocked. "Someone doesn't like us kissing."

The roar slowly faded away. "Bowen, plant a big wet one on Cy."

"My pleasure." He took Cy's face in his hands and dropped a big kiss on his lips.

Again, the deep guttural roar bellowed through the mine. But this time, barely audible, Duff could have sworn he heard "Sodddd-oooo-mite."

"I think this entity is homophobic."

Cy shoved his hands in his pockets, looking around again. "Great! Of all the fucking entities in this world, we've got to get the homophobe."

Duff chuckled. "Let's go, guys. This thing has really piqued my curiosity."

Again, they cautiously ventured deeper into the mineshaft, passing drift after drift without any activity. They turned the next bend in the shaft and hit another dead end.

Duff looked at Cy, who was already studying the rough sketch of the shafts.

"Cy?"

"Nope, it's not supposed to be the end yet. Another twenty or so yards to go."

Lockey studied the wall, and this one was different from the other. It was sloped from his feet almost like a hill reaching to the top of the shaft. He touched it and it was real. "Ah, guys, this looks like a collapse. Look how the wall builds up to the top of the shaft."

"You're right," Bowen acknowledged as he slipped his backpack off of his shoulder. He dug his gloves out of the front compartment, put them on, climbed up to the top of the pile of rocks, and started digging. Duff joined him and the two of them dug for ten minutes or so with Cy and Lockey hauling the larger rocks away from the pile. Bowen unearthed a large boulder he couldn't move alone, so he and Duff worked diligently to dig out around it until they could get their hands behind the rock to try and roll it forward.

They were just about to attempt the maneuver when they heard another loud roar, and the shaft started to rumble and shake. Suddenly they were blown, along with the boulder, off of the pile of rocks by an unseen force. The boulder struck the opposite wall, and Duff and Bowen landed on their asses at the bottom of the rock pile.

Cy watched as Bowen flew through the air. "Bowen!" By the time he reached him, Bowen was already getting to his feet. "Damn, that's going to leave a mark," he whined as he rubbed his ass.

"Tell me about it," Duff said as he wiped blood from the back of his head.

"Duff, you're bleeding, let me see." Lockey started to examine Duff's head.

"No worries, I think it's just a scratch."

"I'll be the judge of that." Lockey dug into the small first aid kit in his backpack and pulled out an alcohol wipe. He cleaned the area and applied a little antibiotic ointment, but by the time he was finished, the bleeding had stopped and Duff was raring to go.

"Good as new," Lockey kissed Duff on the neck and patted his ass.

Again, a very loud roar, but this time they clearly made out "Sodomite."

"Well, if we had any doubt," Cy grunted, "no need to wonder now."

"Guys," Bowen yelled from the top of the rock pile, "we're through."

"Really?" Duff yelled as he climbed up to meet Bowen. Bowen shined his flashlight into the small hole.

"My God, Bowen, you're right. Guys, get up here."

Lockey and Cy climbed up the pile, and together, the four of them cleared away enough rocks and dirt to open a hole about three feet in diameter.

Bowen was the first one through, with Duff quickly on his heels. Lockey climbed back down the pile and retrieved their backpacks and threw them up to Cy, who tossed them through the hole. Cy climbed through next and finally Lockey.

On the other side of the wall, the air was thick, stale, and damp. It was hard to breathe at first, but as fresh air circulated through the mine from their opening, breathing became less cumbersome. They all threw their backpacks over their shoulders, checked their emergency oxygen tanks one more time, and slowly worked their way into the shaft. This end of the shaft seemed to be narrower and had a little less headroom than the part closer to the chamber, but despite the size, it was easily maneuverable. As they approached the first drift, the shaft started to rumble again. They stopped dead in their tracks and waited for the rumble to stop, but it didn't stop. It intensified and pieces of rock started falling from above.

"We'd better get out of here!" Bowen yelled.

Cy grabbed Bowen by the arm and dragged him to the hole and pushed him through. Duff and Lockey were right behind them, struggling to stay upright as the shaft seemed to sway and shift under their feet. Cy helped Lockey and Duff through the hole and climbed up as Bowen reached back, grabbed him by the shirt, and pulled him clear of the opening. They all ran to the chamber, ducking loose pieces of earth and falling rocks. When they reached the chamber, Duff stopped dead in his tracks, staring down at the rappelling line lying in a pile on the ground. *We can't get back up!*

"Motherfucker!" he yelled at the top of his lungs. The shaft suddenly stilled and became silent. "I've had enough of your shit, you cocky son of a bitch." Duff took off running down the mineshaft as fast as he could back toward the opening, climbed the hill, and dove through the hole. When he hit the other side, he tucked, rolled, and landed on his feet. "Show yourself now, you motherfucker." He heard the footsteps of the others running toward him, but he quickly tuned them out as he tried to focus all his energy to force the entity to show itself.

Nothing. He moved his flashlight in unison with his headlamp in every direction and nothing appeared. He ran deeper into the shaft. "Show yourself, you cowardly bastard!" Still nothing. He moved a little farther and sensed the others right behind him. "Get back!" he yelled. "It's me he wants. I'm the only one who can communicate with him."

"You're not doing this alone, Duff," Lockey said. "We're here and we're not leaving you, so get used to it. We're in this together, remember? You and me and Bowen and Cy. We're in this together."

"Dammit," he said under his breath. "Come on, then."

Duff pointed out shadows that were starting to appear along the shaft walls. Shadows other than theirs, rapidly appearing and disappearing. "He's back," Duff whispered. "What do you want from us?" he said in a calm, even voice. "Why won't you show yourself?"

The Mystery of Ruby Lode

The deeper they walked into the shaft, the heavier the air became. There was a flash and their lights went out. They froze, and when their lights came back on, they all screamed because they saw rattlesnakes everywhere, crawling on the floor, slithering over their feet, shaking their rattles as if in defiance. They were striking at their boots and trying to crawl up their legs. Lockey grabbed Duff. "Oh my God, not snakes. I hate snakes."

"Don't be afraid, it's not real," Duff said calmly. "It takes an enormous amount of energy to do what it's doing, and it can't keep it up for very long."

"What is it trying to accomplish?" Lockey asked.

"It's trying to keep us out of this shaft. I just don't know why."

Suddenly there was a flash and the snakes were gone. Lockey closed his eyes and took a deep breath. "Thank you, Jesus," he whispered.

Duff patted him on the shoulder. "Let's go."

They proceeded cautiously, and when they rounded the next bend, they all gasped in unison at what they saw.

There were three seemingly mummified bodies sitting in upright positions with their backs against the shaft wall, holding hands. It was an eerie sight to behold.

"Jesus," Cy whispered. "Is this what it's trying to keep us from seeing?"

Before Duff could answer, Lockey was moving toward the bodies. "Do you think he killed them?"

Duff studied the scene in front of him. "To answer your questions, who the hell knows?"

He followed Lockey over to the bodies and closely inspected them. "Look, everything's still intact."

"It must have been airtight in here." Bowen said.

On Duff's closer inspection, one of the remains seemed to be clutching some type of note, and there was a wooden pencil lying next to it.

Duff carefully slipped the fragile piece of parchment paper from between the fingers and shined his headlamp on it.

"It appears to be the deed to this mine." He started reading aloud: "This deed, made this twelfth day of April, nineteen hundred and fourteen between the county of Boulder and state of Colorado, of the first part, and Counter Stephens, Frink Davis, Hepp Thomas, and Shull Johnson of the county of Boulder in the state of Colorado, of the second part, Witnesses, that the said parties of the first part, for and in consideration of the sum of one hundred dollars to the said parties of the first part hand paid by the said parties of the second part, the receipt whereof is hereby confessed and acknowledged, have remised, released, sold conveyed and quit claim unto the said parties of the second part and their heirs, successors, and assigns, forever, all the right, title, interest, claim, and demand which the said parties of the first part have in and to the following described lot or parcel of land situate, lying and being in the county of Boulder and state of Colorado."

The deed went on to describe the location of the Ruby Lode mining claim, along with the survey number and the acreage.

"It looks like there's something written on the back," Bowen pointed out.

Duff gently flipped the piece of paper over and read aloud again:

"Dear Count,
As I sit here fighting for my last few breaths, I find little comfort in the fact that I will not die alone. Although I'm soothed by the love and devotion Hepp and Shull have shown to one another, it also makes me realize what we could have had, and realizing that makes me hurt so

The Mystery of Ruby Lode

much. The only saving grace is that I'm certain death will come to me very soon and hopefully take with it the emptiness and pain that now haunts me. But even in my current state, with all the sadness and pain consuming me, I can't help but wonder if you're okay and maybe thinking of me.

"Knowing you're just twenty feet away, alone in another part of the shaft, and dying little by little, does nothing but add to my torment. I picture you clearly in my mind with your beautiful blond hair hanging in your face, covering your violet eyes as you gasp for every last breath.

"If I thought you wanted me, I would move heaven and earth to get to you, crawl into your arms and die a happy man. But those are my fantasies, partly brought on by lack of air, but I'll take any happiness I can get, real or not, as long as it erases the thoughts of you from my memory.

"How did it come to this? We've been best friends since we were kids and were supposed to strike it rich in this mine, the very mine that's slowly killing us. I'm sorry I ruined everything by telling you how much I love you. I don't hate you for attacking me. I know I disappointed you. But seeing Hepp and Shull together living quietly as a couple gave me such hope for us. We never spoke of the things that happened between us in the night, but I always thought we felt the same about each other.

"As I lose the ability to grip my pencil, I know death will be so much better than having to live without you. It's getting darker, death is so close now, I can feel it upon me, I keep trying to tell myself that you really do love me and that you know how much I lo...."

"It just stops midsentence," Duff explained.

A deafening silence filled the mineshaft for what seemed like forever. Everyone was trying to process what they'd just heard. The silence was finally broken by the sound of gentle sobs as Cy openly wept. Duff watched Bowen comforting Cy and felt Lockey's arms around him as he offered him a warm embrace.

Duff slipped the note back under Frink's hand, and he and Lockey joined Bowen and Cy. The four of them hugged one another, and when Cy was able to regain his composure, he finally spoke. "That explains why these four guys disappeared shortly after they bought this mine."

"Just twenty feet away," Duff mumbled and flashed his light farther into the shaft. "That means Counter must be over there somewhere."

He rounded the next bend with the others right behind him and flashed his light into the very first drift, and there was Counter, leaning against the wall in much the same way as the others had been. The only difference was, Counter's hands were by his side, still fisted in what Duff assumed was a fit of anger at Frink's admission. "Poor Frink. To die this way, with the person you love so close, yet so far."

Reading Frink's note and learning how he felt about Counter brought back the feeling of longing for Cy for the last ten years. He was happy to have Lockey in his life now, but he couldn't help but think about the parallel lives they'd led.

"Hey, guys," Bowen commented, "does it seem weird to you that three, quite possibly four of these guys were gay, and they died in this mine and then there's us?"

"I was just thinking about the same thing," Cy admitted.

The Mystery of Ruby Lode

Suddenly the once-quiet shaft filled with the eerie sounds of moans as an oily black substance began to seep out of the wall behind the remains.

"Stay back." Duff put his arms up and stepped between the unwelcome visitor and his friends.

They all watched as the thick liquid ran down the wall and attached itself to Counter's dry, brittle bones. The black ooze followed the leg bones down and filled the boots and then made its way back up, forming legs, hips, torso, arms, a neck, and a head until the form of an oily black human body was lying where Counter's remains once lay lifeless. The form began to move, slowly at first, then deliberately as it stood and howled in triumph.

Duff tried to stay as calm as possible. "What do you want with us?"

"Leave here" was very loud and forceful, but "and burn in hell, sodomites" slowly faded and was barely audible.

"He can't keep this up much longer," Duff shared. "It takes too much energy to hold this all together."

The figure raised its fisted hands into the air and howled again as the oily substance started to ooze its way down the bones and gather in a pool around the boots, eventually seeping into the ground.

They all watched in amazement as the exposed bones hobbled over and laid back down in the exact location and position they had been in before the incident.

"Okay, Duff, this is really getting strange," Bowen said, dragging Cy toward the chamber. "I'm gonna try and see if I can get any cell service near the opening. If not, I'm gonna try and climb out of here."

Duff wasn't quite ready to give in. "You guys go ahead and see if you can get out of here. I'm gonna try to make contact one more time. Maybe if it's just me, I can get through to him. Something must have gone down when Frink told Counter he was in love with him, and obviously, Counter reacted badly. The others moved on, but Counter's anger has kept him here, and I need to try and help him cross over."

Lockey stood firm. "I'm not leaving you here alone."

"I'll be fine, I promise. I think all of us being here is affecting my ability to reach him."

Lockey looked a little deflated. "How so?"

"I think I'm too worried about anything happening to you guys to use my abilities to the fullest. I promise you I'll be okay."

"Let's go, Lock. Give him some time alone with this thing. We won't be far, and if we need to, we can get back here within seconds."

Duff saw the reluctance on Lockey's face as he was led away by Bowen and Cy. He watched as they climbed through the opening and back into the main shaft. He walked over to where Frink's, Hepp's, and Shull's remains lay against the wall and sat down next to them. He closed his eyes and tried to reach Counter. After ten minutes, he got nothing and decided to move. *I guess Counter doesn't want to be anywhere near the homos.*

He walked over to where Counter's remains lay and sat across from them. Again, he closed his eyes and tried his best to reach Counter through his mind.

Come on, Counter, I know it's you. Talk to me, damn it. What the hell happened here so long ago that still has you so angry? Was it Frink? Was it Hepp and Shull? You can talk to me!

Duff felt Counter's presence begin to grow. Faintly at first, then it became stronger. Something made him open his eyes, and when he did, his headlamp shone right through a tall, thin, very well-built, blond-headed man pacing in front of him. When the entity stopped and looked at Duff, he saw the most intoxicating eyes he'd ever seen—eyes so blue they were almost violet—and he held their gaze. "Counter, it's okay. Calm down."

"Fuck you!" Counter yelled. "Don't tell me to blasted calm down. I'm surrounded by fucking sodomites and you want me to calm down."

"No one here is going to touch you," Duff assured him. "I just want to help you cross over to be with your friends."

The Mystery of Ruby Lode

"I don't want to be with those sodomites. That's why I stayed here."

"Counter, you've been dead and wandering around this mine for a hundred years. It's time to cross over."

"I can't."

"Why not?"

"Because he's there."

"Who's there?"

Counter didn't answer. After a few seconds, Duff said, "Frink? You can't cross over because Frink's there?"

Counter nodded.

"Counter, everyone's welcome in the light. No one will judge you there."

The shaft started to rumble again and Counter flew into a rage. "I'm no fucking sodomite."

"Okay, okay! Please calm down," Duff begged. "Do you want to tell me what happened the day you died and why you're still so upset about it?"

Counter continued to pace, back and forth, back and forth. "He fucking ruined everything. He couldn't just let things be the way they were. He always wanted more than I could give. I couldn't let him get away with telling people he and I were… well, that we had relations."

Duff's headlamp flickered off and on when Counter roared again. He was getting more and more agitated, and his aura was starting to fade in and out.

"He was in love with you, Counter," Duff whispered. "He wanted to be with you."

"The motherfucker had all I could give, but that wasn't enough. He had to go and run his mouth to his blasted new best friends and ruin everything. Why couldn't things just keep going the way they were?"

"He must have needed more," Duff tried to explain.

"Hepp and Shull, they filled his head with all these 'let's play house' ideas. Frink was happy until we met them."

"Are you sure about that? All this time you spent roaming around this mine, did you ever go over and read the note he left you?"

Counter lowered his head. "I… can't." He hesitated. "I can't see him that way."

"My God, Counter, you did love him."

Duff thought he'd finally gotten through to him, but when Counter looked up again and met Duff's gaze, his blue eyes were gone and a blank stare hung on his face. He clenched his fists again and roared, "I—am—not—a—sodomite!" He ran at Duff, but luckily for him, Counter's energy was dissipating quickly; just before he reached him, Counter disappeared completely.

Cy showed up minutes later. "Boy, it sure sounds like you pissed somebody off."

"I guess I did, but I was so close to making him understand."

"You saw him?"

"Yeah, and it's Counter, just as we suspected. He revealed himself to me right after you guys left. But he won't go to the other part of the shaft because he can't bear to see Frink's remains."

"Then he did love him."

"Yeah, I'm afraid so, but he couldn't deal with being gay."

The shaft rumbled a very weak rumble, but Duff got the point all the same.

Duff explained the rest of his encounter and how it ended.

"I wish I could get him to hear what Frink wrote in that note. Maybe it would help."

"I think the entire thing is incredibly sad," Cy confessed. "I wish things had been different for them."

"Yeah, me too, but what's done is done. If I can just get him to cross over, I'm sure he will feel differently. Hey, let's go and see if we can help the guys get us out of here," Duff suggested.

"What about Counter?"

"He needs to recharge. He was so pissed off at me he used up all of his energy. It'll be a while before we hear from him again."

"You go ahead, Duff; I wanna read that note again. It just about broke my heart."

Duff felt like Cy had something up his sleeve. "I'll just stay with you, then."

"No!" Cy snapped. "I mean… I'd like to be alone."

Duff reluctantly agreed. "I'll be back in a few."

"Okay."

CY WENT back to Frink's remains. He once again slipped the note from its final resting place, looked at it, and walked over to the other part of the shaft and sat down next to Counter's remains. Counter needed to hear what was in that note. Frink deserved at least that much.

He arranged his headlamp so it illuminated the note and started reading aloud. When he finished reading, he wiped the tears away and rested his hand on top of Counter's remains. "He loved you so much, Counter," Cy whispered. "How could you not see he needed more from you? That he needed acknowledgement, love, and support?"

CY COULDN'T see him, but Counter was there all right, standing over him, tears streaming down his face as he heard Frink's last words. His heart was breaking all over again and he longed to see Frink, to be with him. *He still loved me, even after everything I did, everything I put him through. Oh, Frink, I'm so sorry. I want to be with you.* But then he heard the words of his preacher searing back into his memory. *"Sodomites will all burn in hell!"* Fear again took over and he regained his composure. He stood firmly upright, repeating over and over, "I'm not a sodomite. I will not burn in hell," while clenching and releasing his fist repeatedly. *Damn you, sodomite, for bringing all this hurt and pain back to me.* Counter waited for Cy to stand and he dove for him.

CY HAD no idea why this note had affected him so strongly, but now that he'd helped Frink get his final words to Counter, he felt somewhat better. Like maybe he'd helped in some small way. He looked down at Counter's remains again and then up at the ceiling and around the shaft. "Counter, I don't know if you can hear me, but Frink loved you so much. Go to him, don't waste any more time."

Feeling like he'd done what he set out to do, he turned and took his first step. For a split second, his body vibrated and he felt a wisp of air. The hair on the back of his neck stood on end and goose bumps formed all over his body. It was the oddest sensation he'd ever experienced, like some type of energy force was surrounding him. But as quick as the feeling came, it was gone. Suddenly everything went to gray and then eventually to black.

DUFF had just finished bringing the guys up to speed on his latest experience with Counter's spirit when he saw Cy walking into the chamber. He studied him for a second and immediately noticed something was different about him—his stride was off, the way he carried himself was different—but before he could give it any more thought, he was distracted by Lockey, who was standing on his shoulders, shifting his weight. Lockey was trying to support Bowen, who was a quarter of the way up the opening of the shaft trying to climb out, but they weren't having much luck. The shaft was wider at the bottom and there was really nothing to hold on to until he reached

The Mystery of Ruby Lode

the tight spot that had given Cy so much trouble on their first day, and that was still about twelve feet away. With every foot gained, he would lose his grip and slide back down two feet.

With Bowen's next move, he lost it and came sliding down, taking Lockey with him and all three of them landed on their asses. Cy doubled over, burst into laughter, and didn't even bother to help them.

"Thanks for the help, Cyrus," Bowen snapped as he got to his feet and offered a hand to Lockey and then to Duff. "Why are you acting like an ass all of a sudden?"

Cy was still laughing hysterically and Duff was studying him closely. *What is it about him?*

Duff could see how angry Bowen was as he watched him almost beat himself to death dusting off his pants and shirt.

"It looks like we're going to be here until the local authorities come looking for us," he shared. "And that's not going to be for another few hours, at least."

Cy, still trying to compose himself, attempted to speak. "It's not so bad down here."

Everyone turned and glared at him, but he just smiled.

Duff saw the pissed off look Bowen threw at Cy, and then watched as he turned to Lockey. "Let's go. We might as well check out the third shaft while we're here. I don't expect to find much as it was never worked, but as long as we have the time to kill, we should probably document it as well."

"Sure, I'll go with you," Lockey replied.

"And I'll go back and see if I can convince our friend to move on," Duff volunteered.

"What about me?" Cy asked.

Bowen looked at him and just shook his head. "Let's go, Lockey."

Duff, curious to know what was going on with Cy, said, "You can come with me."

"Fine," Cy yelled to Bowen. "If you don't want me, I'll go with Duff." At the end he added in a whisper only Duff could hear, "At least he's still in love with me."

Duff stepped back as if Cy's words had been bullets firing straight into his heart. He felt the blood drain out of his face and turned away so Cy couldn't see exactly what his words had done to him. *Cy, how could you?*

When he felt like he could speak without his voice cracking, he motioned for Cy to follow him. "Let's go."

Cy walked up to him, looked back in Bowen's direction, took Duff by the hand, and dragged him down the shaft to the other section of the mine.

They got to the opening and Duff climbed the hill and went through the opening first. He could feel Cy's eyes staring at his ass the entire time he was crawling through the hole, and it unnerved him terribly. Cy quickly looked away when they walked past the area where Frink's, Hepp's, and Shull's remains were propped up against the wall and made a beeline for Counter's remains. Cy stood silently, eyeing Duff seductively as he paced back and forth, trying to pick up some sense of Counter. After a few minutes of focusing all his energy, he sensed Counter's presence, but it was very weak, almost as if it was being blocked by something. He tried to communicate with him but got no response. He sat down across from Counter's remains, in the same location he'd been in the first time Counter showed himself, and closed his eyes.

He felt goose bumps when Cy brushed against him as he sat down very close, their shoulders and legs pressed against one another. His emotions were suddenly on overload and his hands began to shake from Cy's close proximity, not to mention the sexual vibes he was getting from him. He tried to slow his heartbeat and focus on the task at hand of connecting with Counter's spirit, but his eyes flew open when he felt Cy's hand gently rubbing his thigh, moving closer and closer to his groin.

"Cy! What are you doing?"

"Something I should have done a long time ago. Come on, Duff, you know you want it too."

Duff watched in fear and anticipation as Cy leaned in and pressed their lips together, Cy's tongue seeking entry.

His brain told him no, but his years of unreturned love for Cy told him yes. He froze and felt emotionally defenseless against the onslaught of Cy's advances. No matter how hard he tried, he didn't have the will or the courage to try and stop him.

Cy urged him onto his back and Duff closed his eyes again. *I'm sorry! God help me, I'm so sorry! I can't do this; I've got to stop.*

Cy's gentle kisses on his face and neck were too much for him to fight. But when Cy started rubbing his groin, he momentarily lost all control. His heart raced as his body tingled all over. Every nerve ending was on fire. Cy was seducing him, something he'd dreamed of over and over. Then something flashed in the back of his mind and he saw Lockey back at the inn consoling him after his nightmare and professing his love. Then he saw Bowen, accepting his admissions of loving Cy and trusting him, and suddenly he was disgusted with himself.

"No! Cy, please stop! I don't want to do this. Stop, please!"

He attempted to push Cy away and when he opened his eyes, it wasn't Cy at all. It was Counter's violet eyes staring back at him.

"Counter," he ordered, "get the fuck off of me."

Counter simply smiled, his eyes piercing right through Duff like daggers. Duff fought as hard as he could to break free, but Counter's spirit was stronger than he was. He felt a blow to his head and everything faded to black. Moments later, when he came to, his jeans and underwear were around his ankles and Cy's jeans were down, exposing his rock-hard dick. Counter was holding Duff's hands over his head, using Cy's body to force his knees tightly against his chest as he pushed against his opening. *Oh, God, not again, please not again!*

As Counter forced his way in, Duff heard Lockey yelling in the distance, "Get the fuck off of him, you son of a bitch." Within seconds Lockey was pulling Cy off of him and throwing him up against the wall. Bowen was halfway through the hole when he stopped, not believing what he was seeing. Lockey picked Cy up by the shirt and drew his fist back and let it fly, stopping only when it connected with Cy's jaw.

"No!" Duff yelled, trying to get to his feet. "It's not Cy, it's Counter. Counter's taken over Cy's body!"

Finally making it to his feet, Duff stood and almost fell after getting caught in his jeans and underwear. He pulled everything up as best he could and ran over to Cy. He pushed Lockey out of the way and shook Cy within an inch of his life. "Get out of him, you bastard. It's me you want. Take me. Leave him now!"

Duff looked into Counter's blue eyes and saw nothing but defiance, daring him to try everything he had. "I ain't goin' nowhere," Counter protested.

Duff saw the expression on Lockey and Bowen's faces when they heard Counter's voice coming out of Cy's body. He knew they could only see Cy, but he also knew they realized it was no longer Cy saying the words.

Bowen ran over and grabbed a handful of Cy's shirt and stared right into his eyes. "You get out of him, you sorry good-for-nothing coward. He's mine."

Counter threw his hands up in the air, breaking Bowen's grip and forcing him across the shaft and onto his ass. Lockey ran over to see if Bowen was all right.

"Who in the hell are you calling a coward?" Counter roared.

Bowen stood. "At least I try to protect the people I love. I'm not ashamed of them, and I don't try to hurt them."

Counter's expression changed from anger to hurt as he bowed his head. But then he recovered quickly. "You don't know me or anything about me, you blasted sodomite."

The Mystery of Ruby Lode

"Oh? Don't I?" Bowen shot back. "I think we all know quite a bit about you and how you treated Frink, the person you were supposed to love."

"Stop," Duff yelled and he joined Bowen and Lockey. "We're not going to get Cy back by going down this road."

Counter looked at Duff and smiled. "You ain't gettin' him back at all. I'm stayin' right where I am."

Duff's heart sank. "This is all my fault," he whispered. *I've got to outsmart him somehow.*

Counter laughed, clearly hearing Duff's thoughts. "No sodomite can outsmart me."

Think, Duff, think! You're running out of time. Suddenly Duff caught movement out of the corner of his eye and quickly turned his head in that direction. Standing to his left was the spirit of a handsome, dark-haired young man of nineteen or twenty. He was thin and naturally muscular, with straight, shoulder-length brown hair.

Bowen and Lockey must have seen Duff turn his head and stare in the other direction. "What is it?" Bowen asked.

"Frink. I think Frink's here."

COUNTER sensed a presence he hadn't felt in a very long time. A broad smile appeared on his face as he turned and saw Frink's spirit. He could hardly contain the joy and delight he felt as he gazed upon his long-lost friend.

"Frink?" Counter asked. "Is it really you?"

Frink smiled and nodded.

"Frink, I've missed you so much. I'm so sorry for the way I treated you."

Frink smiled. "That's all behind us now; it's time to come with me. I've waited a hundred years for you to cross over and join me."

"Oh, God, Frink, I've wanted to, so many times. You've got to believe me when I say how many times I've wanted to. But I... I can't."

"You can, just take my hand."

"No. I'm afraid I'll burn in hell," he admitted. "I love you, God help me, I love you, but I don't want to burn in hell. That's why I stayed behind all these years. I am a coward."

"Do I look like I'm burning in hell?" Frink asked. "It was all a lie, Count."

"A lie? But why would someone lie about something like that?"

"Hatred and fear. People say and do all sorts of things in the name of religion."

"But what about judgment day? The Bible says there will be a judgment day."

"There is no judgment day. We are all responsible for the things we do in our lifetime, but no one judges you in the end but yourself."

"But after the way I treated you and Hepp and Shull, I don't deserve to cross over. I don't deserve to be with you, Frink."

"None of that matters."

"It matters to me, Frink. I love you, I never told you, but I love you so much. I just didn't want to be no sodomite."

"And now, Count, what do you want?"

Count stepped out of Cy's body and nervously walked up to Frink. "I want to be with you, if you'll have me."

Frink offered his hand and he willingly accepted it. He looked at Duff and smiled, then together they turned and walked away, disappearing into thin air.

CY STUMBLED back with the sensation of Counter leaving his body. He was left standing alone and feeling very lost. The guys surrounded him very quickly. "Oh, baby, are you okay?" Bowen asked.

The Mystery of Ruby Lode

"What in the hell happened to me? One minute I was sitting there reading Frink's letter and the next I'm standing here exhausted."

"Counter took over your body," Duff explained. "But he's gone now. He's crossed over."

Cy smiled. "He's crossed over?"

"Yep, he's with Frink."

Cy passed out in Bowen's arms. Bowen slid to the ground and they laid Cy down.

"He'll be okay," Duff assured them. "It takes a lot out of you, but he's strong. He'll recover very quickly."

Pretty soon Cy came to, just as Duff had predicted, and they explained everything that had taken place since his possession. They made their way back to the chamber and shortly thereafter, they heard voices. "Mr. McAlister. Can you hear me?"

"We're down here," Bowen called.

A flashlight shined down through the shaft. "Is everyone okay? Does anyone need medical attention?"

"No, we're all fine. Our rappelling line came free and we couldn't get back up the shaft."

"We'll get another line down to you ASAP."

"Thanks," Bowen yelled up to the authorities. He looked to Cy. "Can you make it up, baby?"

"Yeah, sure, I can do it."

A FEW hours later they were back at the inn, showered and sitting cross-legged on Cy and Bowen's bed.

Duff took a deep breath and took Lockey's hand in his. "This has been a trip for the history books."

Cy leaned back against Bowen. "You can say that again."

"Welcome to my world," Duff joked, poking Cy in the ribs.

Cy had been fairly quiet since they got back, and Duff was certain he knew what was on his mind.

He looked at Cy. "It's okay, you know; it wasn't you."

Tears started streaming down Cy's cheeks. "I know it wasn't me, but it was my body. I'm so sorry for the things I said and what I almost did to you."

"But you weren't in control. We all know that, and it's all right."

"Thanks, Duff."

"Obviously, all of this will be our little secret," Lockey said.

"That's probably best," Duff agreed. "No one would believe us anyway."

Cy got up and walked over to his backpack and retrieved his notebook. "First thing tomorrow morning, I'll start working on our report for the Bureau of Land Management, and that will put this expedition officially to bed."

"I don't think it'll be that easy," Lockey commented. "Counter did quite a number on all of us."

Cy sat back down on the bed and scooted up into Bowen's waiting arms. "I think it's a little easier for me because I learned something about my childhood that explained an awful lot about the way I live my life as an adult. But you guys had to come to terms with things that resurfaced, things you thought had long been put to bed."

Bowen wrapped his arms around Cy's shoulders. "I know one thing. When we get back to New York, I'm going to start looking for my birth parents. The truth, whatever it is, has to be better to deal with than not knowing."

Cy brought his hands up and hung them on Bowen's forearms wrapped securely around him. "Whatever we find out about your birth parents, we'll deal with it together, and remember, it won't change who you are." Bowen kissed him on the neck and they leaned back against the headboard together.

"All I know is, you're going to see a new Lockey when we get home," Lockey admitted. "Now that I have this man"—he squeezed Duff's hand—"I'm gonna do everything in my power to keep him. I think I might even try to do a little outreach work at Fort Drum and talk to kids about the effects of being a military brat relocating year after year. Maybe I can help."

"That's a great idea," Duff said. "You'd be so good at that."

There was silence in the room for the next few minutes, but Duff could feel everyone waiting for him to say something. "I'm not sure what I'm going to do about my stepbrother," he finally volunteered. "Prosecuting him now wouldn't change anything, and besides, it's his word against mine."

Lockey gently rubbed Duff's back. "Whatever you decide to do, you know you can count on my support."

"Same here," Bowen said, speaking for himself and Cy.

"Thanks, guys. That means more to me than you'll ever know. But if it's all the same to you, I think I'm ready to turn in."

"Mind if I join you?" Lockey teased.

Duff winked at him. "I was hoping you would."

Everyone stood and they all embraced, knowing this experience had changed them all and forged a bond that could never be broken.

"I love you guys," Duff said as he took Lockey's hand and headed for their room.

"Hey, Duff," Cy said with his arm draped over Bowen's shoulder. "We love you too."

DUFF stripped and climbed into bed. When Lockey finished undressing, he held up the covers as an invitation, which Lockey accepted.

He laid his head on Lockey's chest and listened as Lockey's heartbeat calmed him, giving him the courage to say what he needed to say.

"Um, Lockey?"

Lockey brushed the hair out of Duff's eyes. "Yeah?"

"Thank you for rescuing me from Counter's attack."

Lockey looked down at Duff. "You don't have to thank me for that. I would have killed the motherfucker if he'd hurt you."

"There are so many things wrong with that statement," Duff teased, "I don't know where to start. Firstly, he's already dead, and secondly, you would have killed Cy, not Counter."

"Well, you know what I meant," Lockey stammered.

"I do know what you meant, and I love you for it. But there's something I need to tell you."

"I'm listening."

"Before you guys got there, when it was just Cy and me in the shaft, he started rubbing my leg and kissing me. At that time, I had no reason to know it wasn't Cyrus, and although I knew it was wrong, I didn't make him stop. He was all over me and I… I liked it."

He felt Lockey tense up, inhale deeply, and exhale forcefully. "So what made you stop? I know you tried to stop him because I heard you yelling at him to get off of you. Was that because you realized it wasn't really Cy, but Counter trying to rape you?"

"No! And you've got to believe me when I say this, but it was you. My mind flashed back to the first night we were here and you were comforting me after my nightmare. And the rest of this trip, you've been so supportive and protective of me. It's the first time since my mother died I felt like someone loved me and I no longer felt alone."

Duff leaned up on one elbow and looked Lockey in the eyes. "What I'm trying to say is you saved me both physically and emotionally. I realized Cy had this hold on me I couldn't or wouldn't break. But it wasn't real; it was an illusion of something that could never be. When push came down to shove, it was you I saw in my mind protecting me, not Cy."

Lockey leaned forward until their lips met in a gentle kiss. When he pulled back, Duff saw nothing but love and support in his eyes.

Lockey whispered, "I want nothing more than to protect you and show you how much you're loved and cherished, and I'll spend the rest of my life doing it, if you'll allow me to. I love you, Duff."

Duff didn't know how to respond. He thought he was in love with Lockey, but he wasn't 100 percent sure, and he didn't want to say the words until he was certain without an ounce of doubt.

Lockey must have picked up on the internal struggle and, in true Lockey form, let him off the hook. "No need to respond, baby. I know you've been on an emotional rollercoaster, and I want you to believe it when you finally tell me how much you love me."

Duff smiled as Lockey rolled over on top of him and brought their lips together again. The long, lingering kiss with Lockey's fingers gently caressing his hair made him realize for the first time in a very long time what it felt like to really be loved. His heart was overflowing and he wanted to give Lockey something to show him just how much he cared, and he made the decision with no hesitation.

When the kiss ended, Duff took Lockey's face in his hands. "I want you to make love to me."

Shocked, Lockey froze. "Duff... you said no one's ever touched you there since... well, you know, your stepbrother."

"That's true. But I want the first time since then to be with you. I don't know if I can explain this right, but when I was a kid, it was a horrible experience, and I have those bad memories tucked away in my mind. But right now, today, I'm counting on you to turn those horrible memories into good ones, memories we can hold on to for the rest of our lives. Does that make any sense?"

"It makes perfect sense. A second ago I didn't think I could ever love you more than I already do, but hearing you say those words to me, I think I was wrong."

Duff knew he was doing the right thing for Lockey and for himself. He wanted to show Lockey, not just tell him, how much he meant to him.

Lockey moved slowly and deliberately, removing Duff's underwear and then his own. Duff's nipples were assaulted with kisses and gentle nips as Lockey worked his way down his torso. He gasped when Lockey took him in all the way to the back of his throat in one gulp. "God, that feels so good, Lock. Please don't stop."

Lockey allowed him to slip out of his mouth just long enough to say "never," and then diligently went back to the task at hand. Duff caressed Lockey's hair as he came all the way up and slipped back down until he could feel the back of Lockey's throat against his erection. He felt himself starting to lose it and motioned for Lockey to stop. "If you keep that up, I'm gonna come very soon, and I want to make it last."

When Lockey looked up at him with such loving eyes, he couldn't help himself. "Lockey, please," he whispered. "I've waited so many years; please make love to me now."

Lockey retrieved the lube and a condom from the nightstand and laid them on the bed beside them. He slid down between Duff's legs, gently lifted them, and was rewarded with a beautiful sight. Lockey lowered his head and tenderly licked Duff's opening.

Duff saw stars. The simple act of Lockey's warm wet tongue circling his opening sent his nerve endings into a state of emergency. He had one hand full of Lockey's hair and the other full of sheets, and he couldn't help but move in unison with Lockey's attack.

All his life, he'd associated that area of his body with pain and humiliation and never allowed anyone to show him it could be any different. But now he couldn't help himself as the immense pleasure forced moan after moan out of his throat. Just when he thought he would explode in ecstasy, Lockey's tongue breeched him and set off an entirely different set of sensations. The feeling of Lockey's tongue plunging in and out of him made him painfully hard, and he wasn't sure he could survive the ordeal. When he knew he couldn't take another second of Lockey's tantalizing motions, Lockey stopped. Duff took a deep breath and tried to calm his racing heart. He felt Lockey's gentle movements as he applied the lubricant to both their raging erections. But Duff wasn't prepared for what came next.

Lockey slipped his lubricated finger inside him, and the feeling sent shivers up his spine. His lover moved his finger in and out, slowly preparing him for the onslaught sure to follow. First one finger, then two, and then a third, until Duff was ready. When Lockey removed his fingers, Duff felt empty and longed to feel full again. But that feeling stopped when he felt Lockey pressing against his opening. That simple sensation triggered something in him, and he panicked, holding Lockey at bay. When he closed his eyes, he saw the angry face of his stepbrother kneeling at his open legs, forcing his way in, and it took every ounce of restraint he had not to kick him in the nuts as he'd done the last time Abe tried to rape him. He tried to push the memories away and opened his eyes to see Lockey staring at him with so much concern and love he forgot all about his stepbrother.

"Duff, it's me," he whispered. "We can stop anytime. It doesn't matter to me. I love you."

"It matters to me," Duff said. "I want you, Lockey, all of you. Please."

Lockey pushed in just a little and stopped, giving Duff time to adjust. Duff experienced the all-too-familiar burn. He knew the burn would eventually pass, but it triggered all sorts of memories, and he was determined to replace those memories. He focused on Lockey's eyes and the love he saw there and urged him to continue.

Lockey slid in a little at a time until Duff felt the prickly hair on Lockey's balls tickling his ass. *God, all I need is another sensation to push me over the edge.*

"Move," Duff begged.

Lockey's hips started to slowly draw back and he adjusted to yet another new sensation. Where his stepbrother had been forceful and quick, Lockey was slow and easy, sliding in and out with long, gentle strokes. He was mesmerized by the love pouring out of Lockey's eyes, and he reveled in it. This experience was nothing like he remembered, and as Lockey found his stride, Duff found his own. He started rising into each thrust, pulling Lockey in as far as he could before releasing him and preparing for the next thrust. Suddenly, Lockey brushed against something inside him, and his vision exploded with the brightest light he'd ever seen. "Do that again," Duff pleaded.

Lockey, paying very close attention to his lover's needs, hit the same spot over and over again, sending Duff into a tailspin of emotions and sensations he hadn't been prepared for. He used his hands on Lockey's thighs to pull him in, thrust after thrust, wanting all he could take and all Lockey could give. He felt his release building from deep inside his soul, and although he wanted these sensations to last, he needed this release. He took his dick into his hand and with one stroke, he felt himself clamping down around Lockey as he shot, the first landing next to his face on the pillow. Right before his second shot, he felt Lockey harden just a little more inside him, saw him close his eyes, and heard him scream his name. Duff's next shot landed on his chest and his third on his abdomen until there was nothing left but a dribble sliding down his quivering hand.

He'd never come when his brother was raping him, and he was so thankful, because sharing this for the first time with Lockey was the most intense experience of his life. Lockey leaned forward and their lips met in a blazing kiss. He flinched when Lockey slipped out of him and suddenly longed to feel full again. Duff could feel the tears running down his cheeks as he sorted through a slew of emotions. "Oh, Lock. That was incredible."

"Are… are you okay?" Lockey stuttered. "I hope it was a good experience."

"The best, and that's all thanks to you."

The Mystery of Ruby Lode

Lockey smiled and gave him a quick kiss just before he hopped out of bed, disposed of the condom, and brought in a warm cloth. He wiped Duff clean and again settled in the bed next to him. Duff pulled him close and held on tight. So much had happened to them in the last week, none of it expected and all of it exceptional. Duff had come on this trip, as on all their previous trips, so busy pining away for Cy he hadn't even seen the love existing right under his own nose. But he was leaving Colorado with his demons exorcized, his obsessions put to rest, and a man who truly loved him, one who he was pretty damned sure he loved as well. He closed his eyes and drifted off to sleep, feeling secure and loved for the first time in a very long time.

Epilogue

"Ouch, that's hot," Duff said, brushing his hand against the rack as he pulled a roast out of the oven. Lockey was steaming vegetables and mashing potatoes while they waited for Cy and Bowen to show up for dinner and hopefully bring dessert.

They'd been back in New York for a couple of weeks, and all of them had quickly been sucked back up into their normal lives and routines, except now Duff and Lockey carried out all of their routines together and had spent every waking hour outside of work with one another. They were starting to wonder why they were paying rent on two places when they were at one or the other every night. But as silly as it seemed, they'd both agreed it was a little too soon to start thinking about making that kind of decision.

Duff knew he loved being with Lockey and he knew for sure he loved him, but for so long he'd been used to loving Cyrus, he was gun-shy of saying he was in love with anyone who wasn't Cy. He knew it was stupid, but once he said the L-word, he couldn't take it back, and that meant his fantasy about he and Cyrus being together someday was

The Mystery of Ruby Lode

finally over. He was ready for it to be over and he wanted to be with Lockey, but something was holding him back. He knew his feelings toward Cy had changed back in the mine, but he was clinging to something he logically knew he could never have and really no longer wanted. So why couldn't he commit to Lockey? He'd promised himself and Lockey he wouldn't commit until he could say the words without a shadow of a doubt. And Lockey, true to his word, had never pressured him, but he was starting to feel like there was something fundamentally wrong, and it was bothering him.

They had talked to Cy and Bowen on a regular basis since they'd returned, but they hadn't been able to get together until tonight.

Duff had called the doorman and told him they were expecting Cy and Bowen, so he wasn't surprised to hear a light knock at the door.

Lockey was up to his elbows in mashed potatoes, so Duff stuffed aluminum foil loosely around his roast while it rested and wiped his hands as he went for the door.

"Hey, guys," he said when he opened the door to two handsome men with a bottle of red wine and an apple pie in their hands. "Get your asses in here. It's been two weeks."

"Fuck you," Bowen said as he hugged Duff and made his way into the kitchen.

Cy gave him a tight hug and a kiss on the cheek that, in the past, would have gone right to his groin and left him waiting for his erection to go down before he could move. But nothing happened. Cy was different. His hair was the same, his eyes were the same, he looked the same, but something was different about him.

He and Cy joined Lockey and Bowen in the kitchen. Cy went over to say hello and kissed Lockey's neck; Lockey reciprocated by throwing a spoonful of mashed potatoes over his shoulder and into his face. "Why you little fucker," Cy hissed and looked around the kitchen for something with which to retaliate.

"Don't even think about touching my dinner," Duff said with one hand on his roast and the other on the steaming vegetables. And that started the regular banter Duff had become so used to and depended on so much. Bowen licked most of the potatoes off of Cy's face, and what Bowen didn't get, Cy wiped clean with a paper towel, bitching and moaning about how he was gonna get Lockey back before the night was done.

Over dinner Cy told them everything he'd found out from his parents about his abduction and Bowen shared that he'd started the search for his birth parents.

In turn, Lockey shared that he'd indeed contacted Fort Drum and was in the process of putting together a Saturday morning workshop to help military brats better cope with the things that are out of their control. It was mostly for kids dealing with one or both parents being deployed and bouncing from family member to family member, and those faced with moving every year when their parents were reassigned. And he thought he could work in a little lesson on bullying and what effect that has on kids, young and old. But all in all, he was pretty excited about it.

And lastly, as usual, they all looked at Duff. Lockey knew this, but Duff explained he'd decided against bringing his stepbrother up on charges all these years later. He'd done some research and found out Abe was married and had three kids of his own. Nothing good could come out of these accusations, and again, it was Duff's word against Abe's. But he had decided to write Abe a letter. It would be a way for him to let go, but also a way to let Abe know how he felt about him and that he would never forget what he'd done to him. He'd already written the letter, and it was sitting on his desk addressed and ready to go, but he hadn't decided whether or not he was ever going to send it. He figured the therapy was in the writing, not the sending.

After dinner they moved into the living room while Duff stayed behind in the kitchen to prepare dessert. Like clockwork, the regular banter picked up right where it left off. Duff watched them bitching and griping about one thing or another from the kitchen. He paid special attention to Cy, and for the first time in his life, he finally saw him for what he was: his best friend. The fantasy he'd created and hung onto for so long seemed to have disappeared. In his eyes, Cy had lost whatever he'd seen in him romantically, and now he was just Cyrus Curran, a normal guy with a normal life and seminormal friends.

When the evening was over, they were all standing in the foyer chatting away, with promises of getting together the following week to start planning their next adventure. While Lockey said his goodbyes to Bowen, Duff walked up to Cy. They exchanged knowing glances and Cy opened his arms. Duff stepped into them and they both held on just a little longer than usual, sensing this was the end of one thing and hopefully the beginning of something else.

When he stepped away from the embrace, he felt lighter somehow, as if he'd left whatever was weighing him down with Cy, and the simple thought made him smile. He hugged Bowen; then they walked out of the door.

Later that night when he and Lockey climbed into bed, Lockey lay with his head on Duff's chest, gently caressing his muscles, something Duff had figured out he did when there was something on his mind.

"Do you want to talk about it?"

"About what?"

"Whatever's bothering you."

"How do you know something's bothering me?"

"Because you always rub my chest when you have something on your mind."

"Do not."

"You do too, Lockey. I love the subtle signals you give me because sometimes—let's face it—I'm very dense and could easily miss the signs. But I always know when you rub my chest, I have completely missed something."

"I can't believe I'm that obvious."

"Well, you are, and I love that about you. So are you going to tell me what's bothering you?"

"It's nothing, really. I just saw you staring at Cy earlier this evening, and it got to me a little, that's all. And then when they left, I saw the two of you embracing and sensed something had passed between you."

"You are right on both counts. I was studying Cy this evening, but not for the reasons you think. And I did share an intimate embrace with Cy, but again not for the reason you think."

Lockey lifted his head and their eyes met.

"I realized when Cy walked through the door tonight that something between us had changed. All night I looked for the Cy I used to see, and he's just not there anymore. When you saw us embrace, it was me telling him—or what I once felt for him—good-bye. I think he felt it as well."

Duff's normally strong voice caught when he tried to speak. "I love you, Lockey. I know it now, and I can say it with no fear and be 100 percent sure."

Lockey smiled and laid his head back down on Duff's chest. "Say it again."

"I love you, Lockhart Dawson. I love you with all my heart and soul."

SCOTTY CADE left Corporate America and twenty-five years of marketing and public relations behind to buy an inn & restaurant on the island of Martha's Vineyard with his partner of fourteen years.

He started writing stories as soon as he could read, but only recently for publication. When not at the inn, you can find him on the bow of his boat writing m/m romance novels with his Shetland sheepdog Mavis at his side. Being from the South and a lover of commitment and fidelity, most of his characters find their way to long, healthy relationships, however long it takes them to get there. He believes that, in the end, the boy should always get the boy.

Scotty and his partner are avid boaters and live aboard their boat, spending the summers on Martha's Vineyard and winters in Charleston, SC, and Savannah, GA.

Visit Scotty at http://www.scottycade.com and Scotty Cade on Facebook and Twitter. You can contact him at scotty@scottycade.com.

Romance from SCOTTY CADE

http://www.dreamspinnerpress.com

SCOTTY CADE left Corporate America and twenty-five years of marketing and public relations behind to buy an inn & restaurant on the island of Martha's Vineyard with his partner of fourteen years.

He started writing stories as soon as he could read, but only recently for publication. When not at the inn, you can find him on the bow of his boat writing m/m romance novels with his Shetland sheepdog Mavis at his side. Being from the South and a lover of commitment and fidelity, most of his characters find their way to long, healthy relationships, however long it takes them to get there. He believes that, in the end, the boy should always get the boy.

Scotty and his partner are avid boaters and live aboard their boat, spending the summers on Martha's Vineyard and winters in Charleston, SC, and Savannah, GA.

Visit Scotty at http://www.scottycade.com and Scotty Cade on Facebook and Twitter. You can contact him at scotty@scottycade.com.

Romance from SCOTTY CADE

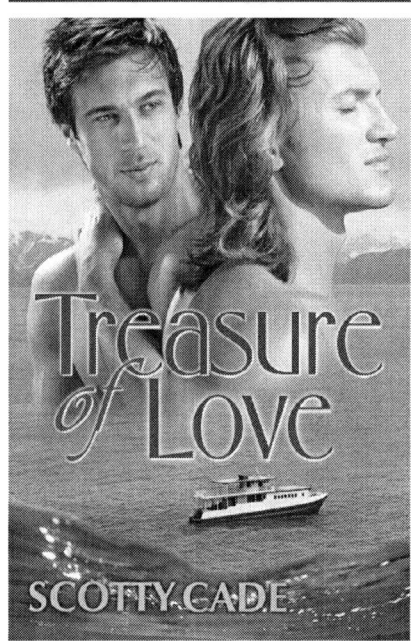

http://www.dreamspinnerpress.com

Romance from SCOTTY CADE

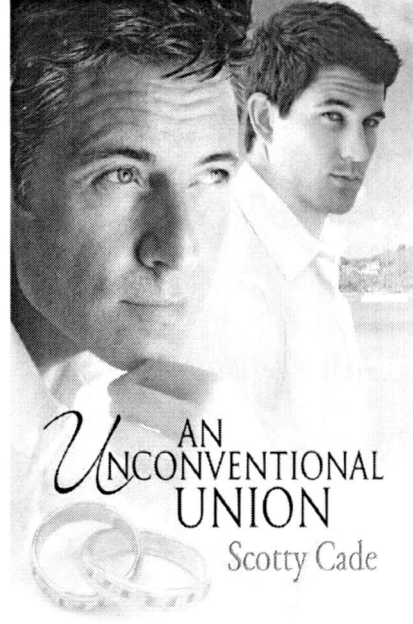

http://www.dreamspinnerpress.com

CPSIA information can be obtained at www.ICGtesting.com
Printed in the USA
LVOW10200090704l3

327975LV00001B/50/P